TELL ME
A RIDDLE

Books by Tillie Olsen

TELL ME A RIDDLE
YONNONDIO: FROM THE THIRTIES
SILENCES
MOTHER TO DAUGHTER; DAUGHTER TO MOTHER

TELL ME
A RIDDLE

BY TILLIE OLSEN

DELTA/SEYMOUR LAWRENCE

A DELTA BOOK
Published by
DELL PUBLISHING
a division of
The Bantam Doubleday Dell Publishing Group, Inc.
666 Fifth Avenue
New York, New York 10103

The contents of this collection appeared originally as follows:

"Hey Sailor, What Ship?" reprinted from *New Campus Writing* published by Bantam Books.

"O Yes" reprinted from *Prairie Schooner* (under the title "Baptism") published by the University of Nebraska Press.

"I Stand Here Ironing" reprinted from *Pacific Spectator* published by the Pacific Coast Committee for the Humanities of the American Council of Learned Societies.

"Tell Me a Riddle" reprinted from *New World Writing 116*.

ISBN: 0-440-55010-6

Reprinted by arrangement with the Author
Printed in the United States of America
One previous Delta edition
New Delta edition—
January 1989

10 9 8 7 6 5 4 3 2 1

FOR MY MOTHER
1885–1956

*The pieces in this collection
are printed in the order of their writing.*

CONTENTS

TELL ME
A RIDDLE

I. I STAND HERE IRONING

1953–1954

I stand here ironing, and what you asked me moves tormented, back and forth with the iron.

"I wish you would manage the time to come in and talk with me about your daughter. I'm sure you can help me understand her. She's a youngster who needs help and whom I'm deeply interested in helping."

"Who needs help." . . . Even if I came, what good would it do? You think because I am her mother I have a key, or that in some way you could use me as a key? She has lived for nineteen years. There is all that life that has happened outside of me, beyond me.

And when is there time to remember, to sift, to weigh, to estimate, to total? I will start and there will be an interruption and I will have to gather it all together again. Or I will become engulfed with all I did or did not do, with what should have been and what cannot be helped.

She was a beautiful baby. The first and only one of our five that was beautiful at birth. You do not guess how new and uneasy her tenancy in her now-loveliness. You did not know her all those years she was thought homely, or see her poring over her baby pictures, making me tell her over and over how beautiful she had been—and would be, I would tell her—and was now, to the seeing eye. But the seeing eyes were few or non-existent. Including mine.

I nursed her. They feel that's important nowadays. I nursed all the children, but with her, with all the fierce rigidity of first motherhood, I did like the books then said. Though her cries battered me to trembling and my breasts ached with swollenness, I waited till the clock decreed.

Why do I put that first? I do not even know if it matters, or if it explains anything.

She was a beautiful baby. She blew shining bubbles of sound. She loved motion, loved light, loved color and music and textures. She would lie on the floor in her blue overalls patting the surface so hard in ecstasy her hands and feet would blur. She was a miracle to me, but when she was eight months old I had to leave her daytimes with the woman downstairs to whom she was no miracle at all, for I worked or looked for work and for Emily's father, who "could no longer endure" (he wrote in his good-bye note) "sharing want with us."

I was nineteen. It was the pre-relief, pre-WPA world of the depression. I would start running as soon as I got

off the streetcar, running up the stairs, the place smell-
ing sour, and awake or asleep to startle awake, when
she saw me she would break into a clogged weeping that
could not be comforted, a weeping I can hear yet.

After a while I found a job hashing at night so I could
be with her days, and it was better. But it came to where
I had to bring her to his family and leave her.

It took a long time to raise the money for her fare
back. Then she got chicken pox and I had to wait longer.
When she finally came, I hardly knew her, walking
quick and nervous like her father, looking like her
father, thin, and dressed in a shoddy red that yellowed
her skin and glared at the pockmarks. All the baby love-
liness gone.

She was two. Old enough for nursery school they said,
and I did not know then what I know now—the fatigue of
the long day, and the lacerations of group life in the kinds
of nurseries that are only parking places for children.

Except that it would have made no difference if I
had known. It was the only place there was. It was the
only way we could be together, the only way I could
hold a job.

And even without knowing, I knew. I knew the
teacher that was evil because all these years it has
curdled into my memory, the little boy hunched in the
corner, her rasp, "why aren't you outside, because Alvin
hits you? that's no reason, go out, scaredy." I knew Emily
hated it even if she did not clutch and implore "don't
go Mommy" like the other children, mornings.

She always had a reason why we should stay home.
Momma, you look sick. Momma, I feel sick. Mom-

ma, the teachers aren't there today, they're sick. Momma, we can't go, there was a fire there last night. Momma, it's a holiday today, no school, they told me.

But never a direct protest, never rebellion. I think of our others in their three-, four-year-oldness—the explosions, the tempers, the denunciations, the demands —and I feel suddenly ill. I put the iron down. What in me demanded that goodness in her? And what was the cost, the cost to her of such goodness?

The old man living in the back once said in his gentle way: "You should smile at Emily more when you look at her." What *was* in my face when I looked at her? I loved her. There were all the acts of love.

It was only with the others I remembered what he said, and it was the face of joy, and not of care or tightness or worry I turned to them—too late for Emily. She does not smile easily, let alone almost always as her brothers and sisters do. Her face is closed and sombre, but when she wants, how fluid. You must have seen it in her pantomimes, you spoke of her rare gift for comedy on the stage that rouses a laughter out of the audience so dear they applaud and applaud and do not want to let her go.

Where does it come from, that comedy? There was none of it in her when she came back to me that second time, after I had had to send her away again. She had a new daddy now to learn to love, and I think perhaps it was a better time.

Except when we left her alone nights, telling ourselves she was old enough.

"Can't you go some other time, Mommy, like tomorrow?" she would ask. "Will it be just a little while you'll be gone? Do you promise?"

The time we came back, the front door open, the clock on the floor in the hall. She rigid awake. "It wasn't just a little while. I didn't cry. Three times I called you, just three times, and then I ran downstairs to open the door so you could come faster. The clock talked loud. I threw it away, it scared me what it talked."

She said the clock talked loud again that night I went to the hospital to have Susan. She was delirious with the fever that comes before red measles, but she was fully conscious all the week I was gone and the week after we were home when she could not come near the new baby or me.

She did not get well. She stayed skeleton thin, not wanting to eat, and night after night she had nightmares. She would call for me, and I would rouse from exhaustion to sleepily call back: "You're all right, darling, go to sleep, it's just a dream," and if she still called, in a sterner voice, "now go to sleep, Emily, there's nothing to hurt you." Twice, only twice, when I had to get up for Susan anyhow, I went in to sit with her.

Now when it is too late (as if she would let me hold and comfort her like I do the others) I get up and go to her at once at her moan or restless stirring. "Are you awake, Emily? Can I get you something?" And the answer is always the same: "No, I'm all right, go back to sleep, Mother."

They persuaded me at the clinic to send her away to a convalescent home in the country where "she can have the kind of food and care you can't manage for her, and you'll be free to concentrate on the new baby." They still send children to that place. I see pictures on the society page of sleek young women planning affairs to raise money for it, or dancing at the affairs, or decorating Easter eggs or filling Christmas stockings for the children.

They never have a picture of the children so I do not know if the girls still wear those gigantic red bows and the ravaged looks on the every other Sunday when parents can come to visit "unless otherwise notified"—as we were notified the first six weeks.

Oh it is a handsome place, green lawns and tall trees and fluted flower beds. High up on the balconies of each cottage the children stand, the girls in their red bows and white dresses, the boys in white suits and giant red ties. The parents stand below shrieking up to be heard and the children shriek down to be heard, and between them the invisible wall "Not To Be Contaminated by Parental Germs or Physical Affection."

There was a tiny girl who always stood hand in hand with Emily. Her parents never came. One visit she was gone. "They moved her to Rose Cottage" Emily shouted in explanation. "They don't like you to love anybody here."

She wrote once a week, the labored writing of a seven-year-old. "I am fine. How is the baby. If I write my leter nicly I will have a star. Love." There never was a star. We wrote every other day, letters she could never hold or keep but only hear read—once. "We simply do not have room for children to keep any personal possessions," they patiently explained when we pieced one Sunday's shrieking together to plead how much it would mean to Emily, who loved so to keep things, to be allowed to keep her letters and cards.

Each visit she looked frailer. "She isn't eating," they told us.

(They had runny eggs for breakfast or mush with lumps, Emily said later, I'd hold it in my mouth and not swallow. Nothing ever tasted good, just when they had chicken.)

It took us eight months to get her released home, and only the fact that she gained back so little of her seven lost pounds convinced the social worker.

I used to try to hold and love her after she came back, but her body would stay stiff, and after a while she'd push away. She ate little. Food sickened her, and I think much of life too. Oh she had physical lightness and brightness, twinkling by on skates, bouncing like a ball up and down up and down over the jump rope, skimming over the hill; but these were momentary.

She fretted about her appearance, thin and dark and foreign-looking at a time when every little girl was supposed to look or thought she should look a chubby blonde replica of Shirley Temple. The doorbell sometimes rang for her, but no one seemed to come and play in the house or be a best friend. Maybe because we moved so much.

There was a boy she loved painfully through two school semesters. Months later she told me how she had taken pennies from my purse to buy him candy. "Licorice was his favorite and I brought him some every day, but he still liked Jennifer better'n me. Why,

Mommy?" The kind of question for which there is no answer.

School was a worry to her. She was not glib or quick in a world where glibness and quickness were easily confused with ability to learn. To her overworked and exasperated teachers she was an overconscientious "slow learner" who kept trying to catch up and was absent entirely too often.

I let her be absent, though sometimes the illness was imaginary. How different from my now-strictness about attendance with the others. I wasn't working. We had a new baby, I was home anyhow. Sometimes, after Susan grew old enough, I would keep her home from school, too, to have them all together.

Mostly Emily had asthma, and her breathing, harsh and labored, would fill the house with a curiously tranquil sound. I would bring the two old dresser mirrors and her boxes of collections to her bed. She would select beads and single earrings, bottle tops and shells, dried flowers and pebbles, old postcards and scraps, all sorts of oddments; then she and Susan would play Kingdom, setting up landscapes and furniture, peopling them with action.

Those were the only times of peaceful companionship between her and Susan. I have edged away from it, that poisonous feeling between them, that terrible balancing of hurts and needs I had to do between the two, and did so badly, those earlier years.

Oh there are conflicts between the others too, each one human, needing, demanding, hurting, taking—but only between Emily and Susan, no, Emily toward Susan that corroding resentment. It seems so obvious on the surface, yet it is not obvious. Susan, the second child, Susan, golden- and curly-haired and chubby, quick and articulate and assured, everything in appearance and manner Emily was not; Susan, not able to resist Emily's precious things, losing or sometimes clumsily breaking them; Susan telling jokes and riddles to company for applause while Emily sat silent (to say to me later: that was *my* riddle, Mother, I told it to Susan); Susan, who for all the five years' difference in age was just a year behind Emily in developing physically.

I am glad for that slow physical development that widened the difference between her and her contemporaries, though she suffered over it. She was too vulnerable for that terrible world of youthful competition, of preening and parading, of constant measuring of yourself against every other, of envy, "If I had that copper hair," "If I had that skin. . . ." She tormented herself enough about not looking like the others, there was enough of the unsureness, the having to be conscious of words before you speak, the constant caring—what are they thinking of me? without having it all magnified by the merciless physical drives.

Ronnie is calling. He is wet and I change him. It is rare there is such a cry now. That time of motherhood is almost behind me when the ear is not one's own but must always be racked and listening for the child cry, the child call. We sit for a while and I hold him, looking out over the city spread in charcoal with its soft aisles of light. *"Shoogily,"* he breathes and curls closer. I carry him back to bed, asleep. *Shoogily.* A funny word, a family word, inherited from Emily, invented by her to say: *comfort.*

In this and other ways she leaves her seal, I say aloud.
And startle at my saying it. What do I mean? What
did I start to gather together, to try and make coherent?
I was at the terrible, growing years. War years. I do not
remember them well. I was working, there were four
smaller ones now, there was not time for her. She had
to help be a mother, and housekeeper, and shopper. She
had to set her seal. Mornings of crisis and near hysteria
trying to get lunches packed, hair combed, coats and
shoes found, everyone to school or Child Care on time,
the baby ready for transportation. And always the paper
scribbled on by a smaller one, the book looked at by
Susan then mislaid, the homework not done. Running
out to that huge school where she was one, she was lost,
she was a drop; suffering over her unpreparedness, stam-
mering and unsure in her classes.

There was so little time left at night after the kids
were bedded down. She would struggle over books, always eating (it was in those years she developed her
enormous appetite that is legendary in our family) and
I would be ironing, or preparing food for the next day,
or writing V-mail to Bill, or tending the baby. Sometimes, to make me laugh, or out of her despair, she
would imitate happenings or types at school.

I think I said once: "Why don't you do something
like this in the school amateur show?" One morning she
phoned me at work, hardly understandable through
the weeping: "Mother, I did it. I won, I won; they gave
me first prize; they clapped and clapped and wouldn't
let me go."

Now suddenly she was Somebody, and as imprisoned
in her difference as she had been in her anonymity.

She began to be asked to perform at other high schools, even in colleges, then at city and statewide affairs. The first one we went to, I only recognized her that first moment when thin, shy, she almost drowned herself into the curtains. Then: Was this Emily? The control, the command, the convulsing and deadly clowning, the spell, then the roaring, stamping audience, unwilling to let this rare and precious laughter out of their lives.

Afterwards: You ought to do something about her with a gift like that—but without money or knowing how, what does one do? We have left it all to her, and the gift has as often eddied inside, clogged and clotted, as been used and growing.

She is coming. She runs up the stairs two at a time with her light graceful step, and I know she is happy tonight. Whatever it was that occasioned your call did not happen today.

"Aren't you ever going to finish the ironing, Mother? Whistler painted his mother in a rocker. I'd have to paint mine standing over an ironing board." This is one of her communicative nights and she tells me everything and nothing as she fixes herself a plate of food out of the icebox.

She is so lovely. Why did you want me to come in at all? Why were you concerned? She will find her way.

She starts up the stairs to bed. "Don't get *me* up with the rest in the morning." "But I thought you were having midterms." "Oh, those," she comes back in, kisses me, and says quite lightly, "in a couple of years when we'll all be atom-dead they won't matter a bit."

She has said it before. She *believes* it. But because I

have been dredging the past, and all that compounds a human being is so heavy and meaningful in me, I cannot endure it tonight.

I will never total it all. I will never come in to say: She was a child seldom smiled at. Her father left me before she was a year old. I had to work her first six years when there was work, or I sent her home and to his relatives. There were years she had care she hated. She was dark and thin and foreign-looking in a world where the prestige went to blondeness and curly hair and dimples, she was slow where glibness was prized. She was a child of anxious, not proud, love. We were poor and could not afford for her the soil of easy growth. I was a young mother, I was a distracted mother. There were the other children pushing up, demanding. Her younger sister seemed all that she was not. There were years she did not let me touch her. She kept too much in herself, her life was such she had to keep too much in herself. My wisdom came too late. She has much to her and probably little will come of it. She is a child of her age, of depression, of war, of fear.

Let her be. So all that is in her will not bloom—but in how many does it? There is still enough left to live by. Only help her to know—help make it so there is cause for her to know—that she is more than this dress on the ironing board, helpless before the iron.

1953–1954

II. HEY SAILOR, WHAT SHIP?

1953–1955

1

The grimy light; the congealing smell of cigarettes that had been smoked long ago and of liquor that had been drunk long ago; the boasting, cursing, wheedling, cringing voices, and the greasy feel of the bar as he gropes for his glass.

Hey Sailor, what ship?

His face flaring in the smoky mirror. The veined gnawing. Wha's it so quiet for? Hey, hit the tune-box. (*Lennie and Helen and the kids.*) Wha time's it anyway? Gotta . . .

Gotta something. Stand watch? No, din't show last night, ain't gonna show tonight, gonna sign off. Out loud: Hell with ship. You got any friends, ship? then hell with your friends. That right, Deeck? And he turns to Deeck for approval, but Deeck is gone. Where's Deeck? Givim five bucks and he blows.

All right, says a nameless one, you're loaded. How's about a buck?

Less one buck. Company. But he too is gone.

And he digs into his pockets to see how much he has left.

Right breast pocket, a crumpled five. Left pants pocket, three, no, four collapsed one-ers. Left jacket pocket, pawn ticket, Manila; card, "When in Managua it's Marie's for Hospitality"; union book; I.D. stuff; trip card; two ones, one five, accordion-pleated together. Right pants pocket, jingle money. Seventeen bucks. And the hands tremble.

Where'd it all go? and he lurches through the past. One hundred and fifty draw yesterday. No, day before, maybe even day 'fore that. Seven for a bottle when cashed the check, twenty to Blackie, thirty-three back to Goldballs, cab to Frisco, thirty-eight, thirty-nine for the jacket and the kicks (new jacket, new kicks, look good to see Lennie and Helen and the kids), twenty-four smackers dues and ten-dollar fine. That fine. . . .

. *Hey,* to the barkeep, one comin' up. And he swizzles it down, pronto. Twenty and seven and thirty-three and thirty-nine. Ten-dollar fine and five to Frenchy at the hall and drinkin' all night with Johnson, don't know how much, and on the way to the paymaster. . . .

The PAYmaster. Out loud, in angry mimicry, with a slight scandihoovian accent, to nobody, nobody at all: Whaddaya think of that? Hafta be able to sign your name or we can't give you your check. Too stewed to sign your name, he says, no check.

Only seventeen bucks. Hey, to the barkeep, how 'bout advancing me fifty? Hunching over the bar, confidential, so he sees the bottles glistening in the depths. See? and he ruffles in his pockets for the voucher, P.F.E., Michael Jackson, thass me, five hundred and twenty-seven and eleven cents. You don' know me? Been here all night, all day. Bell knows me. Get Bell. Been drinkin' here twenty-three years, every time hit Frisco. Ask Bell.

But Bell sold. Forgot, forgot. Took his cushion and moved to Petaluma to raise chickens. Well hell with you. Got any friends? then hell with your friends. Go to Pearl's. (*Not Lennie and Helen and the kids?*) See what's new, or old. Got 'nuf lettuce for *them* babies. But the idea is visual, not physical. Get a bottle first. And he waits for the feeling good that should be there, but there is none, only a sickness lurking.

The Bulkhead sign bile green in the rain. Rain and the street clogged with cars, going-home-from-work cars. Screw 'em all. He starts across. Screech, screech, screech. Brakes jammed on for a block back. M. Norbert Jacklebaum makes 'em stop; said without glee. On to Pearl's. But someone is calling. Whitey, Whitey, get in here you stumblebum. And it is Lennie, a worn likeness of Lennie, so changed he gets in all right, but does not ask questions or answer them. (Are you on a ship or on the beach? How long was the trip? You sick, man, or just stewed? Only three or four days and you're feeling like this? *No*, no stopping for a bottle or to buy presents.)

He only sits while the sickness crouches underneath, waiting to spring, and it muddles in his head, *going to see Lennie and Helen and the kids, no presents for 'em, an' don't even feel good.*

Hey Sailor, what ship?

2

And so he gets there after all, four days and everything else too late. It is an old peaked house on a hill and he has imaged and entered it over and over again, in a thousand various places a thousand various times: on watch and over chow, lying on his bunk or breezing with the guys; from sidewalk beds and doorway shelters, in flophouses and jails; sitting silent at union meetings or waiting in the places one waits, or listening to the Come to Jesus boys.

The stairs are innumerable and he barely makes it to the top. Helen (Helen? so . . . grayed?), Carol, Allie, surging upon him. A fever of hugging and kissing. 'Sabout time, shrills Carol over and over again. 'Sabout time.

Who is real and who is not? Jeannie, taller than Helen suddenly, just standing there, watching. I'm in first grade now, yells Allie, now you can fix my dolly crib, Whitey, it's smashted.

You hit it just right. We've got stew, pressure cooker stuff, but your favorite anyway. How long since you've eaten? And Helen looks at him, kisses him again, and begins to cry.

Mother! orders Jeannie, and marches her into the kitchen.

Whassmatter Helen? One look at me, she begins to cry.

She's glad to see you, you S.O.B.

Whassmatter her? She don't look so good.

You don't look so good either, Lennie says grimly. Better sit for a while.

Mommy oughta quit work, volunteers Carol; she's tired. All the time.

Whirl me round like you always do, Whitey, whirl me round, begs Allie.

Where did you go this time, Whitey? asks Carol. Thought you were going to send me stamps for my collection. Why didn't you come Christmas? Can you help me make a puppet stage?

Cut it, kids, not so many questions, orders Lennie, going up the stairs to wash. Whitey's got to take it easy. We'll hear about everything after dinner.

Your shoes are shiny, says Allie. Becky in my class got new shoes too, Mary Janes, but they're fuzzy. And she kneels down to pat his shoes.

Forgotten, how big the living room was. (And is he really here?) Carol reads the funnies on the floor, her can up in the air. Allie inspects him gravely. You got a new hurt on your face, Whitey. Sing a song, or say Thou Crown 'n Deep. And after dinner can I bounce on you?

Not so many questions, repeats Carol.

Whitey's just gonna sit here. . . . Should go in the kitchen. Help your mommy.

Angry from the kitchen: Well, I don't care. I'm calling Marilyn and tell her not to come; we'll do our homework over there. I'm certainly not going to take a chance and let her come over here.

Shhh, Jeannie, shhh. He beg that, or Helen? The windows are blind with steam, all hidden behind them the city, the bay, the ships. And is it chow time already? He starts up to go, but it seems he lurched and fell, for the sickness springs at last and consumes him. And now Allie is sitting with him. C'mon, sit up and eat, Whitey, Mommy says you have to eat; I'll eat too. Perched beside him, pretty as you please. I'll take a forkful and you take a forkful. You're sloppy, Whitey —for it trickles down his chin. It does not taste; the inside of him burns. She chatters and then the plate is gone and now the city sparkles at him through the windows. Helen and Lennie are sitting there and somebody who looks like somebody he knows.

Chris, reminds Lennie. Don't you remember Chris, the grocery boy when we lived on Aerial way? We told you he's a M.D. now. Fat and a poppa and smug; aren't you smug, Chris?

I almost shipped with you once, Whitey. Don't you remember?

(Long ago. Oh yes, oh yes, but there was no permit to be had; and even if there had been, by that time I didn't have no drag.) Aloud: I remember. You still got the itch? That's why you came round, to get fixed up with a trip card?

I came around to look at you. But that was all he was doing, just sitting there and looking.

Whassmatter? Don't like my looks? Get too beautiful since you last saw me? Handsome new nose 'n everything.

You got too beautiful. Where can I take him, Helen?

Can't take me no place. M. Norbert Jacklebaum's fine.

You've got to get up anyhow, Whitey, so I can make up the couch. Go on, go upstairs with Chris. You're in luck, I even found a clean sheet.

He settles back down on the couch, the lean scarred arms bent under his head for a pillow, the muscles ridged like rope.

He's a lousy doc. Affectionately. Gives me a shot of B-1, sleeping pills, and some bum advice. . . . Whaddaya think of that, he remembered me. Thirteen years and he remembers me.

How could he help remembering you with all the hell his father used to raise cause he'd forget his deliveries listening to your lousy stories? You were his he-ro. . . . How do you like the fire?

Your wood, Whitey, says Helen. Still the stuff you chopped three years back. Needs restacking though.

Get right up and do it. . . . Whadja call him for?

You scared us. Don't forget, your last trip up here was for five weeks in Marine Hospital.

We never saw it hit you like this before, says Lennie. After a five-, six-week tear maybe, but you say this was a couple days. You were really out.

Just catching up on my sleep, tha's all.

There is a new picture over the lamp. Bleached hills,

a fresh-ploughed field, red horses and a blue-overalled figure.

I got a draw coming. More'n five hundred. How's financial situation round here?

We're eating.

Allie say she want me to fix something? Or was it Carol? Those kids are sure. . . . A year'n a half. . . . An effort to talk, for the sleeping pills are already gripping him, and the languid fire, and the rain that has started up again and cannot pierce the windows. How *you* feeling, Helen? She looks more like Helen now.

Keeping my head above water. She would tell him later. She always told him later, when he would be helping in the kitchen maybe, and suddenly it would come out, how she really was and what was really happening, sometimes things she wouldn't even tell Lennie. And this time, the way she looked, the way Lennie looked. . . .

Allie is on the stairs: I had a bad dream, Mommy. Let me stay here till Jeannie comes to bed with me, Mommy. By Whitey.

What was your bad dream, sweetheart?

Lovingly she puts her arms around his neck, curls up. I was losted, she whispers, and instantly is asleep.

He starts as if he has been burned, and quick lest he wake her, begins stroking her soft hair. It is destroying, dissolving him utterly, this helpless warmth against him, this feel of a child—lost country to him and unattainable.

Sure were a lot of kids begging, he says aloud. I think it's worse.

Korea? asks Len.

Never got ashore in Korea. Yokohama, Cebu, Manila.
(The begging children and the lost, the thieving children and the children who were sold.) And he strokes,
strokes Allie's soft hair as if the strokes would solidify,
dense into a protection.

We lay around Pusan six weeks. Forty-three days on
that tub no bigger'n this house and they wouldn't give
us no leave ashore. Forty-three days. Len, I never had
a drop, you believe me, Len?

Felt good most of this trip, Len, just glad to be sailing again, after Pedro. Always a argument. Somebody
says, Christ it's cold, colder'n a whore's heart, and somebody jumps right in and says, colder'n a whore's heart,
hell, you ever in Kobe and broke and Kumi didn't give
you five yen? And then it starts. Both sides.

Len and Helen like those stories. Tell another. Effort.

You should hear this Stover. Ask him, was you ever
in England? and he claps his hands to his head and says,
was I ever in England, Oh boy, was I ever in England,
those limeys, they beat you with bottles. Ask him, was
you ever in Marseilles and he claps his hands to his head
and says, was I ever in Marseilles, Oh boy, was I ever in
Marseilles, them frogs, they kick you with spikes in their
shoes. Ask him, was you ever in Shanghai, and he says,
was I ever in Shanghai, was I ever in Shanghai, man,
they throw the crockery and the stools at you. Thass
everyplace you mention, a different kind of beating.

There was this kid on board, Howie Adams. Gotta
bring him up here. Told him 'bout you. Best people in
the world, I says, always open house. Best kid. Not like

those scenery bums and cherry pickers we got sailing nowadays. Guess what, they made me ship's delegate.

Well, why not? asks Helen; you were probably the best man on board.

A tide of peaceful drowsiness washes over the tumult in him; he is almost asleep, though the veined brown hand still tremblingly strokes, strokes Allie's soft pale hair.

Is that Helen? No, it is Jeannie, so much like Helen of years ago, suddenly there under the hall light, looking in at them all, her cheeks glistening from the rain.

Never saw so many peaceful wrecks in my life. Her look is loving. That's what I want to be when I grow up, just a peaceful wreck holding hands with other peaceful wrecks (For Len and Helen are holding hands). We really fixed Mr. Nickerson. Marilyn did my English, I did her algebra, and her brother Tommy, wrote for us "I will not" five hundred times; then we just tagged on "talk in class, talk in class, talk in class."

She drops her books, kneels down beside Whitey, and using his long ago greeting asks softly, Hey Sailor, what ship?, then turns to her parents. Study in contrasts, Allie's face and Whitey's, where's my camera? Did you tell Whitey I'm graduating in three weeks, do you think you'll be here then, Whitey, and be . . . all right? I'll give you my diploma and write in your name so you can pretend you got through junior high, too. Allie's sure glad you came.

And without warning, with a touch so light, so faint, it seems to breathe against his cheek, she traces a scar. That's a new one, isn't it? Allie noticed. She asked me, does it hurt? Does it?

He stops stroking Allie's hair a moment, starts up again desperately, looks so ill, Helen says sharply: It's late. Better go to bed, Jeannie, there's school tomorrow.

It's late, it's early. Kissing him, Helen, Lennie. Good night. Shall I take my stinky little sister upstairs to bed with me whatever she's doing down here, or shall I leave her for one of you strong men to carry?

Leaning from the middle stair: didn't know you were sick, Whitey, thought you were like . . . some of the other times. From the top stair: see you later, alligators.

Most he wants alone now, alone and a drink, perhaps sleep. And they know. We're going to bed now too. Six comes awful early.

So he endures Helen's kiss too, and Len's affectionate poke. And as Len carries Allie up the stairs, the fire leaps up, kindles Len's shadow so that it seems a dozen bent men cradle a child up endless stairs, while the rain traces on the windows, beseechingly, ceaselessly, like seeking fingers of the blind.

Hey Sailor, what ship? Hey Sailor, what ship?

3

In his sleep he speaks often and loudly, sometimes moans, and toward morning begins the trembling. He wakes into an unshared silence he does not recognize, accustomed so to the various voices of the sea, the multi-pitch of those with whom sleep as well as work and food is shared, the throb of engines, churn of the propeller; or hazed through drink, the noises of the street, or the thin walls like ears—magnifying into lives as senseless as one's own.

Here there is only the whisper of the clock (motor by which this house runs now) and the sounds of oneself.

The trembling will not cease. In the kitchen there is a note:

Bacon and eggs in the icebox and coffee's made. The kids are coming straight home from school to be with you. DON'T go down to the front, Lennie'll take you tomorrow. Love.

Love.

The row of cans on the cupboard shelves is thin. So things are still bad, he thinks, no money for stocking up. He opens all the doors hopefully, but if there is a bottle, it is hidden. A long time he stares at the floor, goes out into the yard where fallen rain beads the grasses that will be weeds soon enough, comes back, stares at his dampened feet, stares at the floor some more (needs scrubbing, and the woodwork can stand some too; well, maybe after I feel better), but there are no dishes in the sink, it is all cleaner than he expected.

Upstairs, incredibly, the beds are made, no clothes crumpled on the floor. Except in Jeannie's and Allie's room: there, as remembered, the dust feathers in the corners and dolls sprawl with books, records, and underwear. Guess she'll never get it clean. And up rises his old vision, of how he will return here, laden with groceries, no one in the littered house, and quickly, before they come, straighten the upstairs (the grime in the washbasin), clean the downstairs, scrub the kitchen floor, wash the hills of dishes, put potatoes in and light the oven, and when they finally troop in say, calmly, Helen, the house is clean, and there's steak for dinner.

Whether it is this that hurts in his stomach or the burning chill that will not stop, he dresses himself hastily, arguing with the new shoes that glint with a life all their own. On his way out, he stops for a minute to gloss his hand over the bookcase. Damn good paint job, he says out loud, if I say so myself. Still stands up after fourteen years. Real good that red backing Helen liked so much 'cause it shows above the books.

Hey Sailor, what ship?

4

It is five days before he comes again. A cabbie precedes him up the stairs, loaded with bundles. Right through, right into the kitchen, man, directs Whitey, feeling good, oh quite obviously feeling good. The shoes are spotted now, he wears a torn Melton in place of the new jacket. Groceries, he announces heavily, indicating the packages plopped down. Steak. Whatever you're eating, throw it out.

Didn't I tell you they're a good-looking bunch? triumphantly indicating around the table. 'Cept that Lennie hyena over there. Go on, man, take the whole five smackers.

Don't let him go, Whitey, I wanta ride in the cab, screams Allie.

To the top of the next hill and back, it's a winding curly round and round road, yells Carol.

I'll go too, says Jeannie.

Shut up, Lennie explodes, let the man go, he's working. Sit down, kids. Sit down, Whitey.

Set another plate, Jeannie, says Helen.

An' bring glasses. Got coke for the kids. We gonna have a drink.

I want a cab ride, Allie insists.

Wait till your mean old bastard father's not lookin'. Then we'll go.

Watch the language, Whitey, there's a gentleman present, says Helen. Finish your plate, Allie.

Thass right. Know who the gen'lmun is? I'm the gen'lmun. The world, says Marx, is divided into two classes. . . .

Seafaring gen'lmun and shoreside bastards, choruses Lennie with him.

Why, Daddy! says Jeannie.

You're a mean ole bassard father, says Allie.

Thass right, tell him off, urges Whitey. Hell with waitin' for glasses. Down the ol' hatch.

My class is divided by marks, says Carol, giggling helplessly at her own joke, and anyway what about ladies? Where's *my* drink? Down the hatch.

I got presents, kids. In the kitchen.

Where they'll stay, warns Helen, till after dinner. Just keep sitting.

Course Jeannie over there doesn't care 'bout a present. She's too grown up. Royal highness doesn't even kiss old Whitey, just slams a plate at him.

Fork, knife, spoon too, says Jeannie, why don't you use them?

Good chow, Helen. But he hardly eats, and as they clear the table, he lays down a tenner.

All right, sailor, says Lennie, put your money back.

I'll take it, says Carol, if it's an orphan.

If you get into the front room quick, says Lennie, you won't have to do the dishes.

Who gives a shit about the dishes?

Watch it, says Helen.

Whenja start doin' dishes in this house after dinner anyway?

Since we got organized, says Lennie, always get things done when they're supposed to be. Organized the life out of ourselves. That's what's the matter with Helen.

Well, when you work, Helen starts to explain.

Lookit Daddy kiss Mommy.

Give me my present and whirl me, Whitey, whirl me, demands Allie.

No whirling. Jus' sat down, honey. How'd it be if I bounce you? Lef' my ol' lady in New Orleans with twenny-four kids and a can of beans.

Guess you think 'cause I'm ten I'm too big to bounce any more, says Carol.

Bounce everybody. Jeannie. Your mom. Even Lennie.

> *What is life*
> *Without a wife* (bounce)
> *And a home* (bounce bounce)
> *Without a baby?*

Hey, Helen, bring in those presents. Tell Jeannie,

don't come in here, don't get a present. Jeannie, play those marimba records. Want marimba. Feel good, sure feel good. Hey, Lennie, get your wild ass in here, got things to tell you. Leave the women do the work.

Wild ass, giggles Allie.

Jeannie gets mad when you talk like that, says Carol. Give us our presents and let's have a cab ride and tell us about the time you were torpedoed.

Tell us Crown 'n Deep.

Go tell yourself. I'm gonner have a drink.

Down the hatch, Whitey.

Down the hatch.

Better taper off, guy, says Lennie, coming in. We want to have an evening.

Tell Helen bring the presents. She don't hafta be jealous. I got money for her. Helen likes money.

Upstairs, says Helen, they'll get their presents upstairs. After they're ready for bed. There's school tomorrow.

First we'll get them after dinner and now after we're ready for bed. That's not fair, wails Allie.

I never showed him my album yet, says Carol. He never said Crown n' Deep yet.

It isn't fair. We never had our cab ride.

Whitey'll be here tomorrow, says Helen.

Maybe he won't, says Carol. He's got a room rented, he told me. Six weeks' rent in advance and furnished with eighteen cans of beans and thirty-six cans of sardines. All shored up, says Whitey. Somebody called Deeck stays there too.

Lef' my wile ass in New Orleans, twenty-four kids

and a present of beans, chants Allie, bouncing herself up and down on the couch. And it's not *fair*.

Say good night to them, Whitey, they'll come down in their nightgowns for a good-night kiss later.

Go on, kids. Mind your momma, don't be like me. An' here's a dollar for you an' a dollar for you. An' a drink for me.

But Lennie has taken the bottle. Whass ɹ er, doncha like to see me feelin' good? Well, screw ʝou, brother, I'm supplied, and he pulls a pint out of his pocket.

Listen, Whitey, says Jeannie, I've got some friends coming over and . . . Whitey, please, they're not used to your kind of language.

That so? 'Scuse me, your royal highness. Here's ten dollars, your royal highness. Help you forgive?

Please go sit in the kitchen. Please, Daddy, take him in the kitchen with you.

Jeannie, says Lennie, give him back the money.

He gave it to me, it's mine.

Give it back.

All right. Flinging it down, running up the stairs.

Quit it, Whitey, says Lennie.

Quit what?

Throwing your goddam money around. Where do you think you are, down on the front?

'S better down on the front. You're gettin' holier than the dago pope.

I mean it, guy. And tone down that language. Let's have the bottle.

No. Into the pocket. Do *you* good to feel good for a change. You 'n Helen look like you been through the meat grinder.

Silence.

Gently: Tell me about the trip, Whitey.

Good trip. Most of the time. 'Lected me ship's delegate.

You told us.

Tell you 'bout that kid, Howie? Best kid. Got my gear off the ship and lef' it down at the hall for me. Whaddaya think of that?

(Oh feeling good, come back, come back.)

Jeannie in her hat and coat. Stiffly. Thank you for the earrings, Whitey.

Real crystals. Best . . . Lennie, 'm gonna give her ten dollars. For treat her friends. After all, ain't she my wife?

Whitey, do I have to hear that story again? I was four years old.

Again? (He had told the story so often, as often as anyone would listen, whenever he felt good, and always as he told it, the same shy happiness would wing through him, how when she was four, she had crawled into bed beside him one morning, announcing triumphantly to her mother: I'm married to Whitey now, I don't have to sleep by myself any more.) Sorry, royal highness, won't mention it. How's watch I gave you, remember?

(Not what he means to say at all. Remember the love I gave you, the worship offered, the toys I mended and made, the questions answered, the care for you, the pride in you.)

I lost the watch, remember? 'I was too young for such expensive presents.' You keep talking about it because that's the only reason you give presents, to buy people to be nice to you and to yak about the presents when you're drunk. Here's your earrings too. I'm going outside to wait for my friends.

Jeannie! It is Helen, back down with the kids. Jeannie, come into the kitchen with me.

Jeannie's gonna get heck, says Carol. Geeeee, down the hatch. Wish *I* could swallow so long. Is my dresser set solid gold like it looks?

Kiss the dolly you gave me, says Allie. She's your grandchild now. You kiss her too, Daddy. I bet she was the biggest dolly in the store.

Your dolly can't talk. Thass good, honey, that she can't talk.

Here's my album, Whitey. It's got a picture of you. Is that really you, Whitey? It don't look like. . . .

Don't look, he says to himself, closing his eyes. Don't look. But it is indelible. Under the joyful sun, proud sea, proud ship as background, the proud young man, glistening hair and eyes, joyful body, face open to life, unlined. Sixteen? Seventeen? Close it up, he says, M. Norbert Jacklebaum never saw the guy. Quit punchin' me.

Nobody's punchin' you Whitey, says Allie. You're feeling your face.

Tracing the scars, the pits and lines, the battered nose; seeking to find.

Your name's Michael Jackson, Whitey, why do you always say Jacklebaum? marvels Allie.

Tell Crown 'n Deep. I try to remember it and I never can, Carol says, softly. Neither can Jeannie. Tell Crown 'n Deep, tell how you learnt it. If you feel like. Please.

Oh yes, he feels like. *When there is November in my soul,* he begins. No, wrong one.

Taking the old proud stance. The Valedictory, written the dawn 'fore he was executed by Jose Rizal, national hero of the Philippines. Taught me by Li'l Joe Roco, not much taller'n you, Jeannie, my first shipmate.

I'm Carol, not Jeannie.

Li'l Joe. Never got back home, they were puttin' the hatch covers on and . . . I only say it when it's special. Jose Rizal: El Ultimo Adiós. Known as The Valedictory, 1896.

> *Land I adore, farewell.* . . .
> *Our forfeited garden of Eden,*
> *Joyous I yield up for thee my sad life*
> *And were it far brighter,*
> *Young or rose-strewn, still would I give it.*
>
> *Vision I followed from afar,*
> *Desire that spurred on and consumed me,*
> *Beautiful it is to fall,*
> *That the vision may rise to fulfillment.*

Go on, Whitey.

> *Little will matter, my country,*
> *That thou shouldst forget me.*
> *I shall be speech in thy ears, fragrance and color,*
> *Light and shout and loved song.* . . .

Inaudible.

O crown and deep of my sorrows,
I am leaving all with thee, my friends, my love,
Where I go are no tyrants. . . .

He stands there, swaying. Say good night, says
Lennie. Whitey'll tell it all some other time. . . . Here,
guy, sit down.

And in the kitchen.
You know how he talks. How can you let him? In
front of the little kids.
They don't hear the words, they hear what's behind
them. There are worse words than cuss words, there
are words that hurt. When Whitey talks like that, it's
everyday words; the men he lives with talk like that,
that's all.
Well, not the kind of men I want to know. I don't
go over to anybody's house and hear words like that.
Jeannie, who are you kidding? You kids use them all.
That's different, that's being grown-up, like smoking.
And he's so drunk. Why didn't Daddy let me keep the
ten dollars? It would mean a lot to me, and it doesn't
mean anything to him.
It's his money. He worked for it, it's the only power
he has. We don't take Whitey's money.
Oh no. Except when he gives it to you.
When he was staying with us, when they were rock-
ing chair, unemployment checks, it was different. He
was sober. It was his share.
He's just a Howard Street wino now—why don't you

and Daddy kick him out of the house? He doesn't belong here.

Of course he belongs here, he's a part of us, like family. . . . Jeannie, this is the only house in the world he
can come into and be around people without having to
pay.

Somebody who brings presents and whirls you around
and expects you to jump for his old money.

Remember how good he's been to you. To us. Jeannie,
he was only a few years older than you when he started
going to sea.

Now you're going to tell me the one about how he
saved Daddy's life in the strike in 1934.

He knows more about people and places than almost
anyone I've ever known. You can learn from him.

When's he like that any more? He's just a Howard
Street wino, that's all.

Jeannie, I care you should understand. You think
Mr. Norris is a tragedy, you feel sorry for him because
he talks intelligent and lives in a nice house and has
quiet drunks. You've got to understand.

Just a wino. Even if it's whisky when he's got the
money. Which isn't for long.

To understand.

*In the beginning there had been youth and the joy
of raising hell and that curious inability to take a
whore unless he were high with drink.*

*And later there were memories to forget, dreams
to be stifled, hopes to be murdered.*

Know who was the ol' man on the ship? Blackie Karns, Kissass Karns hisself.

Started right when you did, Whitey.

Oh yes. (A few had nimbly, limberly clambered up.) Remember in the war he was the only one of us would wear his braid uptown? That one year I made mate? Know how to deal with you, Jackson, he says. No place for you on the ships any more, he says. My asshole still knows more than all of you put together, I says.

What was it all about, Whitey?

Don' remember. Rotten feed. Bring him up a plate and say, eat it yourself. Nobody gonna do much till we get better. We got better.

This kid, overtime comin' to him. Didn't even wanta beef about it. I did it anyway. Got fined by the union for takin' it up. M. Norbert Jacklebaum fined by the union, "conduct unbefitting ship's delegate" says the Patrolman, "not taking it up through proper channels." (His old fine talent for mimicry jutting through the blurred-together words.)

These kids, these cherry pickers, they don't realize how we got what we got. Beginnin' to lose it, too. Think anybody backed me up, Len? Just this Howie and a scenery bum, Goldballs, gonna write a book. Have you in it, Jackson, he says, you're a real salt.

Understand. The death of the brotherhood. Once, once an injury to one is an injury to all. Once, once they had to live for each other. And whoever came off the ship fat shared, because that was the only way of survival for all of them, the easy sharing, the knowing that when you needed, waiting for a trip card to come up, you'd be staked.

Now it was a dwindling few, and more and more of them winos, who shipped sometimes or had long ago irrevocably lost their book for nonpayment of dues.

Hey, came here to feel good. Down the hatch. Hell with you. You got any friends? Hell with your friends.

Helen is back. So you still remember El Ultimo, Whitey. Remember when we first heard Joe recite it?

I remember.

Remember too much, too goddam much. For twenty-three years, the watery shifting: many faces, many places.

But more and more, certain things the same. The gin mills and the cathouses. The calabozas and jails and stockades. More and more New York and Norfolk and New Orleans and Pedro and Frisco and Seattle like the foreign ports: docks, clip joints, hockshops, cathouses, skid rows, the Law and the Wall: only so far shall you go and no further, uptown forbidden, not your language, not your people, not your country.

Added sometimes now, the hospital.

What's going to happen with you, Whitey?

What I care? Nobody hasta care what happens to M. Jacklebaum.

How can we help caring, Whitey? Jesus, man, you're a chunk of our lives.

Shove it, Lennie. So you're a chunk of my life. So?

Understand. Once they had been young together.

To Lennie he remained a tie to adventure and a world in which men had not eaten each other; and the pleasure, when the mind was clear, of chewing over with that tough mind the happenings of the times or the queernesses of people, or laughing over the mimicry.

To Helen he was the compound of much help given, much support: the ear to hear, the hand that understands how much a scrubbed floor, or a washed dish, or a child taken care of for a while, can mean.

They had believed in his salvation, once. Get him away from the front where he has to drink for company and for a woman. The torn-out-of-him confession, the drunken end of his eight-months-sober try to make a go of it on the beach—don't you see, I can't go near a whore unless I'm lit?

If they could know what it is like now, so casual as if it were after thirty years of marriage.

Later, the times he had left money with them for plans: fix his teeth, buy a car, get into the Ship Painters, go see his family in Chi. But soon enough the demands for the money when the drunken need was on him, so that after a few tries they gave up trying to keep it for him.

Later still, the first time it became too much and Lennie forbade the house to him unless he were "O.K." —"because of the children."

Now the decaying body, the body that was betraying him. And the memories to forget, the dreams to be stifled, the hopeless hopes to be murdered.

What's going to happen with you, Whitey? Helen repeats. I never know if you'll be back. If you'll be able to be back.

He tips the bottle to the end. Thirstily he thinks: Deeck and his room where he can yell or sing or pound and Deeck will look on without reproach or pity or anguish.

I'm goin' now.

Wait, Whitey. We'll drive you. Want to know where you're shacked, anyway.

Go own steam. Send you a card.

By Jeannie, silent and shrunken into her coat. He passes no one in the streets. They are inside, each in his slab of house, watching the flickering light of television. The sullen fog is on his face, but by the time he has walked to the third hill, it has lifted so he can see the city below him, wave after wave, and there at the crest, the tiny house he has left, its eyes unshaded. After a while they blur with the myriad others that stare at him so blindly.

Then he goes down.

Hey Sailor, what ship?
Hey Marinero, what ship?

San Francisco 1953, 1955

For Jack Eggan   *1915–1938*
Seaman. Volunteer, Abraham Lincoln
   Brigade
Killed in the Loyalist retreat
   across the Ebro, Spain.

III. O YES

1956

1

They are the only white people there, sitting in the
dimness of the Negro church that had once been a
corner store, and all through the bubbling, swelling,
seething of before the services, twelve-year-old Carol
clenches tight her mother's hand, the other resting
lightly on her friend, Parialee Phillips, for whose baptism she has come.

The white-gloved ushers hurry up and down the
aisle, beckoning people to their seats. A jostle of people.
To the chairs angled to the left for the youth choir, to
the chairs angled to the right for the ladies' choir, even
up to the platform, where behind the place for the
dignitaries and the mixed choir, the new baptismal
tank gleams—and as if pouring into it from the ceiling,
the blue-painted River of Jordan, God standing in the
waters, embracing a brown man in a leopard skin and
pointing to the letters of gold:

REJOICE

```
      D            L
   O      IS    O
 G                 V
                    E
```

I AM THE WAY   THE TRUTH   THE LIFE

At the clear window, the crucified Christ embroidered on the starched white curtain leaps in the wind of the sudden singing. And the choirs march in. Robes of wine, of blue, of red.

"We stands and sings too," says Parialee's mother, Alva, to Helen; though already Parialee has pulled Carol up. Singing, little Lucinda Phillips fluffs out her many petticoats; singing, little Bubbie bounces up and down on his heels.

Any day now I'll reach that land of freedom,
Yes, o yes
Any day now, know that promised land

The youth choir claps and taps to accent the swing of it. Beginning to tap, Carol stiffens. "Parry, look. Somebody from school."

"Once more once," says Parialee, in the new way she likes to talk now.

"Eddie Garlin's up there. He's in my math."

"Couple cats from Franklin Jr. chirps in the choir. No harm or alarm."

Anxiously Carol scans the faces to see who else she might know, who else might know her, but looks quickly down to Lucinda's wide skirts, for it seems Eddie looks back at her, sullen or troubled, though it is hard to tell, faced as she is into the window of curtained sunblaze.

I know my robe will fit me well
I tried it on at the gates of hell

If it were a record she would play it over and over, Carol thought, to untwine the intertwined voices, to search how the many rhythms rock apart and yet are one glad rhythm.

When I get to heaven gonna sing and shout
Nobody be able to turn me out

"That's Mr. Chairback Evans going to invocate," Lucinda leans across Parry to explain. "He don't invoke good like Momma."

"Shhhh."

"Momma's the only lady in the church that invocates. She made the prayer last week. (Last month, Lucy.) I made the children's 'nouncement last time. (That was way back Thanksgiving.) And Bubbie's 'nounced too. Lots of times."

"Lucy-inda. SIT!"

Bible study announcements and mixed-choir practice announcements and Teen Age Hearts meeting announcements.

If Eddie said something to her about being there, worried Carol, if he talked to her right in front of somebody at school.

Messengers of Faith announcements and Mamboettes announcement and Committee for the Musical Tea.

Parry's arm so warm. Not realizing, starting up the

old game from grade school, drumming a rhythm on
the other's arm to see if the song could be guessed.
"Parry, guess."

But Parry is pondering the platform.

The baptismal tank? "Parry, are you scared . . . the
baptizing?"

"This cat? No." Shaking her head so slow and scorn-
ful, the barrette in her hair, sun fired, strikes a long rail
of light. And still ponders the platform.

New Strangers Baptist Church invites you and Canaan
Fair Singers announcements and Battle of Song and
Cosmopolites meet. "O Lord, I couldn't find no ease," a
solo. The ladies' choir:

> O what you say seekers, o what you say seekers,
> Will you never turn back no more?

The mixed choir sings:

> Ezekiel saw that wheel of time
> Every spoke was of humankind . . .

And the slim worn man in the pin-stripe suit starts
his sermon On the Nature of God. How God is long-
suffering. Oh, how long he has suffered. Calling the
roll of the mighty nations, that rose and fell and now
are dust for grinding the face of Man.

O voice of drowsiness and dream to which Carol does
not need to listen. As long ago. Parry warm beside her
too, as it used to be, there in the classroom at Mann
Elementary, and the feel of drenched in sun and dimness and dream. Smell and sound of the chalk wearing
itself away to nothing, rustle of books, drumming tattoo
of Parry's fingers on her arm: *Guess.*

And as the preacher's voice spins happy and free, it is the used-to-be play-yard. Tag. Thump of the volley ball. Ecstasy of the jump rope. Parry, do pepper. Carol, do pepper. Parry's bettern Carol, Carol's bettern Parry. . . .

Did someone scream?

It seemed someone screamed—but all were sitting as before, though the sun no longer blared through the windows. She tried to see up where Eddie was, but the ushers were standing at the head of the aisle now, the ladies in white dresses like nurses or waitresses wear, the men holding their white-gloved hands up so one could see their palms.

"And God is Powerful," the preacher was chanting. "Nothing for him to scoop out the oceans and pat up the mountains. Nothing for him to scoop up the miry clay and create man. Man, I said, create Man."

The lady in front of her moaned *"O yes"* and others were moaning *"O yes."*

"And when the earth mourned the Lord said, Weep not, for all will be returned to you, every dust, every atom. And the tired dust settles back, goes back. Until that Judgment Day. That great day."

"O yes."

The ushers were giving out fans. Carol reached for one and Parry said: "What *you* need one for?" but she took it anyway.

"You think Satchmo can blow; you think Muggsy can blow; you think Dizzy can blow?" He was straining to an imaginary trumpet now, his head far back and his voice coming out like a trumpet.

"Oh Parry, he's so good."

"Well. Jelly jelly."

"Nothing to Gabriel on that great getting-up morning. And the horn wakes up Adam, and Adam runs to wake up Eve, and Eve moans; Just one more minute, let me sleep, and Adam yells, Great Day, woman, don't you know it's the Great Day?"

"Great Day, Great Day," the mixed choir behind the preacher rejoices:

> *When our cares are past*
> *when we're home at last . . .*

"And Eve runs to wake up Cain." Running round the platform, stooping and shaking imaginary sleepers, "and Cain runs to wake up Abel." Looping, scalloping his voice—"Grea-aaa-aat Daaaay." All the choirs thundering:

> *Great Day*
> *When the battle's fought*
> *And the victory's won*

Exultant spirals of sound. And Carol caught into it (Eddie forgotten, the game forgotten) chanting with Lucy and Bubbie: *"Great Day."*

"Ohhhhhhhhhh," his voice like a trumpet again, "the re-unioning. Ohhhhhhhhh, the rejoicing. After the ages immemorial of longing."

Someone *was* screaming. And an awful thrumming sound with it, like feet and hands thrashing around, like a giant jumping of a rope.

"Great Day." And no one stirred or stared as the ushers brought a little woman out into the aisle, scream-

ing and shaking, just a little shrunk-up woman, not
much taller than Carol, the biggest thing about her her
swollen hands and the cascades of tears wearing her face.

The shaking inside Carol too. Turning and trembling to ask: "What . . . that lady?" But Parry still
ponders the platform; little Lucy loops ,the chain of
her bracelet round and round; and Bubbie sits placidly,
dreamily. Alva Phillips is up fanning a lady in front of
her; two lady ushers are fanning other people Carol cannot see. And her mother, her mother looks in a sleep.

Yes. He raised up the dead from the grave. He made
old death behave.

Yes. Yes. From all over, hushed.   *O Yes*
He was your mother's rock. Your father's mighty tower.
And he gave us a little baby. A little baby to love.

I am so glad
Yes, your friend, when you're friendless. Your father
when you're fatherless. Way maker. Door opener.

Yes
When it seems you can't go on any longer, he's there.
You can, he says, you can.

Yes
And that burden you been carrying—ohhhhh that
burden—not for always will it be. No, not for always.

Stay with me, Lord
I will put my Word in you and it is power. I will put
my Truth in you and it is power.

O Yes
Out of your suffering I will make you to stand as a
stone. A tried stone. Hewn out of the mountains of ages
eternal.

Ohhhhhhhhhhh. Out of the mire I will lift your feet. Your tired feet from so much wandering. From so much work and wear and hard times.

Yes

From so much journeying—and never the promised land. And I'll wash them in the well your tears made. And I'll shod them in the gospel of peace, and of feeling good. Ohhhhhhhhh.

O Yes.

Behind Carol, a trembling wavering scream. Then the thrashing. Up above, the singing:

> *They taken my blessed Jesus and flogged him to*
>   *the woods*
> *And they made him hew out his cross and they*
>   *dragged him to Calvary*
>
> *Shout brother, Shout shout shout. He never cried*
>   *a word.*

Powerful throbbing voices. Calling and answering to each other.

> *They taken my blessed Jesus and whipped him up*
>   *the hill*
> *With a knotty whip and a raggedy thorn he never*
>   *cried a word*
> *Shout, sister. Shout shout shout. He never cried a*
>   *word.*

> *Go tell the people the Saviour has risen*
> *Has risen from the dead and will live forevermore*
>   *And won't have to die no more.*
> *Halleloo.*

Shout, brother, shout
We won't have to die no more!

A single exultant lunge of shriek. Then the thrashing. All around a clapping. Shouts with it. The piano whipping, whipping air to a froth. Singing now.

I once was lost who now am found
Was blind who now can see

On Carol's fan, a little Jesus walked on wondrously blue waters to where bearded disciples spread nets out of a fishing boat. If she studied the fan—became it—it might make a wall around her. If she could make what was happening (*what* was happening?) into a record small and round to listen to far and far as if into a seashell—the stamp and rills and spirals all tiny (but never any screaming).

wade wade in the water

Jordan's water is chilly and wild
I've got to get home to the other side
God's going to trouble the waters

The music leaps and prowls. Ladders of screamings. Drumming feet of ushers running. And still little Lucy fluffs her skirts, loops the chain on her bracelet; still Bubbie sits and rocks dreamily; and only eyes turn for an instant to the aisle as if nothing were happening. "Mother, let's go home," Carol begs, but her mother holds her so tight. Alva Phillips, strong Alva, rocking too and chanting, *O Yes.* No, do not look.

Wade,
Sea of trouble all mingled with fire
Come on my brethren it's time to go higher
Wade wade

The voices in great humming waves, slow, slow (when did it become the humming?), everyone swaying with it too, moving like in slow waves and singing, and up where Eddie is, a new cry, wild and open, "O help me, Jesus," and when Carol opens her eyes she closes them again, quick, but still can see the new known face from school (not Eddie), the thrashing, writhing body struggling against the ushers with the look of grave and loving support on their faces, and hear the torn, tearing cry: "Don't take me away, life everlasting don't take me away."

And now the rhinestones in Parry's hair glitter wicked; the white hands of the ushers, fanning, foam in the air; the blue-painted waters of Jordan swell and thunder; Christ spirals on his cross in the window—and she is drowned under the sluice of the slow singing and the sway.

So high up and forgotten the waves and the world, so stirless the deep cool green and the wrecks of what had been. Here now Hostess Foods, where Alva Phillips works her nights—but different from that time Alva had taken them through before work, for it is all sunken under water, the creaking loading platform where they had left the night behind; the closet room where Alva's swaddles of sweaters, boots, and cap hung, the long hall lined with pickle barrels, the sharp freezer door swinging open.

Bubbles of breath that swell. A gulp of numbing air. She swims into the chill room where the huge wheels of cheese stand, and Alva swims too, deftly oiling each machine: slicers and wedgers and the convey, that at her touch start to roll and grind. The light of day blazes up and Alva is holding a cup, saying: Drink this, baby.

"DRINK IT." Her mother's voice and the numbing air demanding her to pay attention. Up through the waters and into the car.

"That's right, lambie, now lie back." Her mother's lap.

"Mother."

"Shhhhh. You almost fainted, lambie."

Alva's voice. "You gonna be all right, Carol . . . Lucy, I'm telling you for the last time, you and Buford get back into that church. Carol is *fine*."

"Lucyinda, if I had all your petticoats I could float." Crying. "Why didn't you let me wear my full skirt with the petticoats, Mother."

"Shhhhh, lamb." Smoothing her cheek. "Just breathe, take long deep breaths."

". . . How you doing now, you little ol' consolation prize?" It is Parry, but she does not come in the car or reach to Carol through the open window: "No need to cuss and fuss. You going to be sharp as a tack, Jack."

Answering automatically: "And cool as a fool."

Quick, they look at each other.

"Parry, we have to go home now, don't we, Mother?

I almost fainted, didn't I, Mother? . . . Parry, I'm
sorry I got sick and have to miss your baptism."

"Don't feel sorry. I'll feel better you not there to
watch. It was our mommas wanted you to be there, not
me."

"Parry!" Three voices.

"Maybe I'll come over to play kickball after. If you
feeling better. Maybe. Or bring the pogo." Old shared
joys in her voice. "Or any little thing."

In just a whisper: "Or any little thing. Parry. Good-
bye, Parry."

And why does Alva have to talk now?

"You all right? You breathin' deep like your momma
said? Was it too close 'n hot in there? Did something
scare you, Carrie?"

Shaking her head to lie, "No."

"I blames myself for not paying attention. You not
used to people letting go that way. Lucy and Bubbie,
Parialee, they used to it. They been coming since they
lap babies."

"Alva, that's all right. Alva. Mrs. Phillips."

"You *was* scared. Carol, it's something to study about.
You'll feel better if you understand."

Trying not to listen.

"You not used to hearing what people keeps inside,
Carol. You know how music can make you feel things?
Glad or sad or like you can't sit still? That was religion
music, Carol."

"I have to breathe deep, Mother said."

"Not everybody feels religion the same way. Some it's

in their mouth, but some it's like a hope in their blood, their bones. And they singing songs every word that's real to them, Carol, every word out of they own life. And the preaching finding lodgment in their hearts."

The screaming was tuning up in her ears again, high above Alva's patient voice and the waves lapping and fretting.

"Maybe somebody's had a hard week, Carol, and they locked up with it. Maybe a lot of hard weeks bearing down."

"Mother, my head hurts."

"And they're home, Carol, church is home. Maybe the only place they can feel how they feel and maybe let it come out. So they can go on. And it's all right."

"Please, Alva. Mother, tell Alva my head hurts."

"Get Happy, we call it, and most it's a good feeling, Carol. When you got all that locked up inside you."

"Tell her we have to go home. It's all right, Alva. Please, Mother. Say good-bye. Good-bye."

When I was carrying Parry and her father left me, and I fifteen years old, one thousand miles away from home, sin-sick and never really believing, as still I don't believe all, scorning, for what have it done to help, waiting there in the clinic and maybe sleeping, a voice called: Alva, Alva. So mournful and so sweet: Alva. Fear not, I have loved you from the foundation of the universe. And a little small child tugged on my dress. He was carrying a parade stick, on the end of it a star that outshined the sun. Follow me, he said. And the real sun went down and he hidden his stick. How dark it was, how dark. I

*could feel the darkness with my hands. And when I
could see, I screamed. Dump trucks run, dumping
bodies in hell, and a convey line run, never ceasing with
souls, weary ones having to stamp and shove them along,
and the air like fire. Oh I never want to hear such
screaming. Then the little child jumped on a motorbike
making a path no bigger than my little finger. But first
he greased my feet with the hands of my momma when
I was a knee baby. They shined like the sun was on
them. Eyes he placed all around my head, and as I jour-
neyed upward after him, it seemed I heard a mourning:
"Mama Mama you must help carry the world." The rise
and fall of nations I saw. And the voice called again
Alva Alva, and I flew into a world of light, multitudes
singing, Free, free, I am so glad.*

2

Helen began to cry, telling her husband about it.

"You and Alva ought to have your heads examined,
taking her there cold like that," Len said. "All right,
wreck my best handkerchief. Anyway, now that she's
had a bath, her Sunday dinner. . . ."

"And been fussed over," seventeen-year-old Jeannie
put in.

"She seems good as new. Now *you* forget it, Helen."

"I can't. Something . . . deep happened. If only I or
Alva had told her what it would be like. . . . But I
didn't realize."

You don't realize a lot of things, Mother, Jeannie
said, but not aloud.

"So Alva talked about it after instead of before. Maybe it meant more that way."

"Oh Len, she didn't listen."

"You don't know if she did or not. Or what there was in the experience for her. . . ."

Enough to pull that kid apart two ways even more, Jeannie said, but still not aloud.

"I was so glad she and Parry were going someplace together again. Now that'll be between them too. Len, they really need, miss each other. What happened in a few months? When I think of how close they were, the hours of makebelieve and dressup and playing ball and collecting. . . ."

"Grow up, Mother." Jeannie's voice was harsh. "Parialee's collecting something else now. Like her own crowd. Like jivetalk and rhythmandblues. Like teachers who treat her like a dummy and white kids who treat her like dirt; boys who think she's really something and chicks who. . . ."

"Jeannie, I know. It hurts."

"Well, maybe it hurts Parry too. Maybe. At least she's got a crowd. Just don't let it hurt Carol though, 'cause there's nothing she can do about it. That's all through, her and Parialee Phillips, put away with their paper dolls."

"No, Jeannie, no."

"It's like Ginger and me. Remember Ginger, my best friend in Horace Mann. But you hardly noticed when it happened to us, did you . . . because she was white? Yes, Ginger, who's got two kids now, who quit school year before last. Parry's never going to finish either.

What's she got to do with Carrie any more? They're going different places. Different places, different crowds. And they're sorting. . . ."

"Now wait, Jeannie. Parry's just as bright, just as capable."

"They're in junior high, Mother. Don't you know about junior high? How they sort? And it's all where you're going. Yes and Parry's colored and Carrie's white. And you have to watch everything, what you wear and how you wear it and who you eat lunch with and how much homework you do and how you act to the teacher and what you laugh at. . . . And run with your crowd."

"It's that final?" asked Len. "Don't you think kids like Carol and Parry can show it doesn't *have* to be that way."

"They can't. They can't. They don't let you."

"No need to shout," he said mildly. "And who do you mean by 'they' and what do you mean by 'sorting'?"

How they sort. A foreboding of comprehension whirled within Helen. What was it Carol had told her of the Welcome Assembly the first day in junior high? The models showing How to Dress and How Not to Dress and half the girls in their loved new clothes watching their counterparts up on the stage—*their* straight skirt, their sweater, their earrings, lipstick, hairdo— "How Not to Dress," "a bad reputation for your school." It was nowhere in Carol's description, yet picturing it now, it seemed to Helen that a mute cry of violated dignity hung in the air. Later there had been a story of going to another Low 7 homeroom on an errand and seeing a teacher trying to wipe the forbidden lipstick off a girl who was fighting back and cursing. Helen could hear Carol's frightened, self-righteous tones: ". . . and I hope they expel her; she's the kind that gives Franklin Jr. a bad rep; she doesn't care about anything and always gets into fights." Yet there was nothing in these incidents to touch the heavy comprehension that waited. . . . Homework, the wonderings those times Jeannie and Carol needed help: "What if there's no one at home to give the help, and the teachers with their two hundred and forty kids a day can't or don't or the kids don't ask and they fall hopelessly behind, what then?"—but this too was unrelated. And what had it been that time about Parry? "Mother, Melanie and Sharon won't go if they know Parry's coming." Then of course you'll go with Parry, she's been your friend longer, she had answered, but where was it they were going and what had finally happened? Len, my head hurts, she felt like saying, in Carol's voice in the car, but Len's eyes were grave on Jeannie who was saying passionately:

"If you think it's so goddam important why do we have to live here where it's for real; why don't we move to Ivy like Betsy (yes, I know, money), where it's the deal to be buddies, in school anyway, three coloured kids and their father's a doctor or judge or something big wheel and one always gets elected President or head song girl or something to prove oh how we're democratic. . . . What do you want of that poor kid anyway? Make up your mind. Stay friends with Parry—but be one of the kids. Sure. Be a brain—but not a square. Rise on up, college prep, but don't get separated. Yes, stay one of the kids but. . . ."

"Jeannie. You're not talking about Carol at all, are

you, Jeannie? Say it again. I wasn't listening. I was trying to think."

"She will not say it again," Len said firmly, "you look about ready to pull a Carol. One a day's our quota. And you, Jeannie, we'd better cool it. Too much to talk about for one session. . . . Here, come to the window and watch the Carol and Parry you're both all worked up about."

In the wind and the shimmering sunset light, half the children of the block are playing down the street. Leaping, bouncing, hallooing, tugging the kites of spring. In the old synchronized understanding, Carol and Parry kick, catch, kick, catch. And now Parry jumps on her pogo stick (the last time), Carol shadowing her, and Bubbie, arching his body in a semicircle of joy, bounding after them, high, higher, higher.

And the months go by and supposedly it is forgotten, except for the now and then when, self-important, Carol will say: I really truly did nearly faint, didn't I, Mother, that time I went to church with Parry?

And now seldom Parry and Carol walk the hill together. Melanie's mother drives by to pick up Carol, and the several times Helen has suggested Parry, too, Carol is quick to explain: "She's already left" or "She isn't ready; she'll make us late."

And after school? Carol is off to club or skating or library or someone's house, and Parry can stay for kickball only on the rare afternoons when she does not have to hurry home where Lucy, Bubbie, and the cousins wait to be cared for, now Alva works the four to twelve-thirty shift.

No more the bending together over the homework.
All semester the teachers have been different, and rarely
Parry brings her books home, for where is there space
or time and what is the sense? And the phone never
rings with: what you going to wear tomorrow, are you
bringing your lunch, or come on over, let's design some
clothes for the Katy Keane comic-book contest. And
Parry never drops by with Alva for Saturday snack to or
from grocery shopping.

And the months go by and the sorting goes on and
seemingly it is over until that morning when Helen
must stay home from work, so swollen and feverish is
Carol with mumps.

The afternoon before, Parry had come by, skimming up the stairs, spilling books and binders on the
bed: Hey frail, lookahere and wail, your momma
askin for homework, what she got against YOU?
. . . looking quickly once then not looking again and
talking fast. . . . Hey, you bloomed. You gonna be
your own pumpkin, hallowe'en? Your momma know
yet it's mu-umps? And lumps. Momma says: no dis-
tress, she'll be by tomorrow morning see do you need
anything while your momma's to work. . . . (Singing: *whole lotta shakin goin on.*) All your 'signments
is inside; Miss Rockface says the teachers to write
'em cause I mightn't get it right all right.

But did not tell: Does your mother work for Carol's
mother? Oh, you're neighbors! Very well, I'll send
along a monitor to open Carol's locker but you're
only to take these things I'm writing down, nothing
else. Now say after me: Miss Campbell is trusting

me to be a good responsible girl. And go right to
Carol's house. After school. Not stop anywhere on
the way. Not lose anything. And only take. What's
written on the list.

You really gonna mess with that book stuff? Sign on
mine says do-not-open-until-eX-mas. . . . That Mrs.
Fernandez doll she didn't send nothin, she was the
only, says feel better and read a book to report if you
feel like and I'm the most for takin care for you; she's
my most, wish I could get her but she only teaches
'celerated. . . . Flicking the old read books on the
shelf but not opening to mock-declaim as once she
used to . . . Vicky, Eddie's g.f. in Rockface office,
she's on suspended for sure, yellin to Rockface: you
bitchkitty don't you give me no more bad shit. That
Vicky she can sure sling-ating-ring it. Staring out the
window as if the tree not there in which they had hid
out and rocked so often. . . . For sure. (*Keep mo-o-
vin.*) Got me a new pink top and lilac skirt. Look
sharp with this purple? Cinching in the wide belt
as if delighted with what newly swelled above and
swelled below. Wear it Saturday night to Sweet's,
Modernaires Sounds of Joy, Leroy and Ginny and me
goin if Momma'll stay home. IF. (*Shake my baby
shake*). How come old folks still likes to party? Huh?
Asking of Rembrandt's weary old face looking from
the wall. How come (softly) you long-gone you.
Touching her face to his quickly, lightly. NEXT
mumps is your buddybud Melanie's turn to tote your
stuff. *I'm* gettin the hoovus goovus. Hey you so un-
neat, don't care what you bed with. Removing the

books and binders, ranging them on the dresser one
by one, marking lipstick faces—bemused or mocking
or amazed—on each paper jacket. Better. Fluffing out
smoothing the quilt with exaggerated energy. Any
little thing I can get, cause I gotta blow. Tossing up
and catching their year-ago, arm-in-arm graduation
picture, replacing it deftly, upside down, into its
mirror crevice. Joe. Bring you joy juice or fizz water
or kickapoo? Adding a frown line to one bookface.
Twanging the paper fishkite, the Japanese windbell
overhead, setting the mobile they had once made of
painted eggshells and decorated straws to twirling
and rocking. And is gone.

She talked to the lipstick faces after, in her fever,
tried to stand on her head to match the picture, twirled
and twanged with the violent overhead.

Sleeping at last after the disordered night. Having
surrounded herself with the furnishings of that world
of childhood she no sooner learned to live in comfort-
ably, then had to leave.

The dollhouse stands there to arrange and rearrange;
the shell and picture card collections to re-sort and remember; the population of dolls given away to little
sister, borrowed back, propped all around to dress and
undress and caress.

She has thrown off her nightgown because of the
fever, and her just budding breast is exposed where
she reaches to hold the floppy plush dog that had been
her childhood pillow.

Not for anything would Helen have disturbed her.

Except that in the unaccustomedness of a morning at home, in the bruised restlessness after the sleepless night, she clicks on the radio—and the storm of singing whirls into the room:

> . . . *of trouble all mingled with fire*
> *Come on my brethern we've got to go higher*
> *Wade, wade.* . . .

And Carol runs down the stairs, shrieking and shrieking. "Turn it off, Mother, turn it off." Hurling herself at the dial and wrenching it so it comes off in her hand.

"Ohhhhh," choked and convulsive, while Helen tries to hold her, to quiet.

"Mother, why did they sing and scream like that?"

"At Parry's church?"

"Yes." Rocking and strangling the cries. "I hear it all the time." Clinging and beseeching. ". . . What was it, Mother? Why?"

Emotion, Helen thought of explaining, *a characteristic of the religion of all oppressed peoples, yes your very own great-grandparents*—thought of saying. And discarded.

Aren't you now, haven't you had feelings in yourself so strong they had to come out some way? ("what howls restrained by decorum")—thought of saying. And discarded.

Repeat Alva: *hope . . . every word out of their own life. A place to let go. And church is home.* And discarded.

The special history of the Negro people—history?—

just you try living what must be lived every day—
thought of saying. And discarded.

And said nothing.

And said nothing.

And soothed and held.

"Mother, a lot of the teachers and kids don't like
Parry when they don't even know what she's like.
Just because. . ." Rocking again, convulsive and
shamed. "And I'm not really her friend any more."

No news. Betrayal and shame. Who betrayed? Whose
shame? Brought herself to say aloud: "But may be
friends again. As Alva and I are."

The sobbing a whisper. "That girl Vicky who got
that way when I fainted, she's in school. She's the one
keeps wearing the lipstick and they wipe it off and she's
always in trouble and now maybe she's expelled.
Mother."

"Yes, lambie."

"She acts so awful outside but I remember how she
was in church and whenever I see her now I have to
wonder. And hear . . . like I'm her, Mother, like I'm
her." Clinging and trembling. "Oh why do I have to
feel it's happening to me too?

"Mother, I want to forget about it all, and not care,—
like Melanie. Why can't I forget? Oh why is it like it is
and why do I have to care?"

Caressing, quieting.

Thinking: *caring asks doing. It is a long baptism into
the seas of humankind, my daughter. Better immersion
than to live untouched. . . . Yet how will you sustain?*

Why is it like it is?

Sheltering her daughter close, mourning the illusion of the embrace.

And why do I have to care?

While in her, her own need leapt and plunged for the place of strength that was not—where one could scream or sorrow while all knew and accepted, and gloved and loving hands waited to support and understand.

For Margaret Heaton, who always taught

IV. TELL ME
A RIDDLE

"These Things Shall Be"

(1956–1960)

1

For forty-seven years they had been married. How deep back the stubborn, gnarled roots of the quarrel reached, no one could say—but only now, when tending to the needs of others no longer shackled them together, the roots swelled up visible, split the earth between them, and the tearing shook even to the children, long since grown.

Why now, why now? wailed Hannah.

As if when we grew up weren't enough, said Paul.

Poor Ma. Poor Dad. It hurts so for both of them, said Vivi. They never had very much; at least in old age they should be happy.

Knock their heads together, insisted Sammy; tell

'em: you're too old for this kind of thing; no reason not to get along now.

Lennie wrote to Clara: They've lived over so much together; what could possibly tear them apart?

Something tangible enough.

Arthritic hands, and such work as he got, occasional. Poverty all his life, and there was little breath left for running. He could not, could not turn away from this desire: to have the troubling of responsibility, the fretting with money, over and done with; to be free, to be *care*free where success was not measured by accumulation, and there was use for the vitality still in him.

There was a way. They could sell the house, and with the money join his lodge's Haven, cooperative for the aged. Happy communal life, and was he not already an official; had he not helped organize it, raise funds, served as a trustee?

But she—would not consider it.

"What do we need all this for?" he would ask loudly, for her hearing aid was turned down and the vacuum was shrilling. "Five rooms" (pushing the sofa so she could get into the corner) "furniture" (smoothing down the rug) "floors and surfaces to make work. Tell me, why do we need it?" And he was glad he could ask in a scream.

"Because I'm use't."

"Because you're use't. This is a reason, Mrs. Word Miser? Used to can get unused!"

"Enough unused I have to get used to already. . . . Not enough words?" turning off the vacuum a moment to hear herself answer. "Because soon enough we'll need only a little closet, no windows, no furniture, nothing to make work, but for worms. Because now I want room. . . . Screech and blow like you're doing, you'll need that closet even sooner. . . . Ha, again!" for the vacuum bag wailed, puffed half up, hung stubbornly limp. "This time fix it so it stays; quick before the phone rings and you get too important-busy."

But while he struggled with the motor, it seethed in him. Why fix it? Why have to bother? And if it can't be fixed, have to wring the mind with how to pay the repair? At the Haven they come in with their own machines to clean your room or your cottage; you fish, or play cards, or make jokes in the sun, not with knotty fingers fight to mend vacuums.

Over the dishes, coaxingly: "For once in your life, to be free, to have everything done for you, like a queen."

"I never liked queens."

"No dishes, no garbage, no towel to sop, no worry what to buy, what to eat."

"And what else would I do with my empty hands? Better to eat at my own table when I want, and to cook and eat how I want."

"In the cottages they buy what you ask, and cook it how you like. *You* are the one who always used to say: better mankind born without mouths and stomachs than always to worry for money to buy, to shop, to fix, to cook, to wash, to clean."

"How cleverly you hid that you heard. I said it then because eighteen hours a day I ran. And you never

scraped a carrot or knew a dish towel sops. Now—for
you and me—who cares? A herring out of a jar is
enough. But when *I* want, and nobody to bother." And
she turned off her ear button, so she would not have to
hear.

But as *he* had no peace, juggling and rejuggling the
money to figure: how will I pay for this now?; prying
out the storm windows (there they take care of this);
jolting in the streetcar on errands (there I would not
have to ride to take care of this or that); fending the
patronizing relatives just back from Florida (at the
Haven it matters what one is, not what one can afford),
he gave *her* no peace.

"Look! In their bulletin. A reading circle. Twice a
week it meets."

"Haumm," her answer of not listening.

"A reading circle. Chekhov they read that you like,
and Peretz. Cultured people at the Haven that you
would enjoy."

"Enjoy!" She tasted the word. "Now, when it pleases
you, you find a reading circle for me. And forty years
ago when the children were morsels and there was a
Circle, did you stay home with them once so I could
go? Even once? You trained me well. I do not need
others to enjoy. Others!" Her voice trembled. "Because
you want to be there with others. Already it makes me
sick to think of you always around others. Clown,
grimacer, floormat, yesman, entertainer, whatever they
want of you."

And now it was he who turned on the television loud
so he need not hear.

Old scar tissue ruptured and the wounds festered anew. Chekhov indeed. She thought without softness of that young wife, who in the deep night hours while she nursed the current baby, and perhaps held another in her lap, would try to stay awake for the only time there was to read. She would feel again the weather of the outside on his cheek when, coming late from a meeting, he would find her so, and stimulated and ardent, sniffing her skin, coax: "I'll put the baby to bed, and you—put the book away, don't read, don't read."

That had been the most beguiling of all the "don't read, put your book away" her life had been. Chekhov indeed!

"Money?" She shrugged him off. "Could we get poorer than once we were? And in America, who starves?"

But as still he pressed:

"Let me alone about money. Was there ever enough? Seven little ones—for every penny I had to ask—and sometimes, remember, there was nothing. But always *I* had to manage. Now *you* manage. Rub your nose in it good."

But from those years she had had to manage, old humiliations and terrors rose up, lived again, and forced her to relive them. The children's needings; that grocer's face or this merchant's wife she had had to beg credit from when credit was a disgrace; the scenery of the long blocks walked around when she could not pay; school coming, and the desperate going over the old to see what could yet be remade; the soups of meat bones begged "for-the-dog" one winter. . . .

Enough. Now they had no children. Let *him* wrack his head for how they would live. She would not exchange her solitude for anything. *Never again to be forced to move to the rhythms of others.*

For in this solitude she had won to reconciled peace.

Tranquillity from having the empty house no longer an enemy, for it stayed clean—not as in the days when it was her family, the life in it, that had seemed the enemy: tracking, smudging, littering, dirtying, engaging her in endless defeating battle—and on whom her endless defeat had been spewed.

The few old books, memorized from rereading; the pictures to ponder (the magnifying glass superimposed on her heavy eyeglasses). Or when she wishes, when he is gone, the phonograph, that if she turns up very loud and strains, she can hear: the ordered sounds and the struggling.

Out in the garden, growing things to nurture. Birds to be kept out of the pear tree, and when the pears are heavy and ripe, the old fury of work, for all must be canned, nothing wasted.

And her one social duty (for she will not go to luncheons or meetings) the boxes of old clothes left with her, as with a life-practised eye for finding what is still wearable within the worn (again the magnifying glass superimposed on the heavy glasses) she scans and sorts —this for rag or rummage, that for mending and cleaning, and this for sending away.

Being able at last to live within, and not move to the

rhythms of others, as life had forced her to: denying;
removing; isolating; taking the children one by one;
then deafening, half-blinding—and at last, presenting
her solitude.

And in it she had won to a reconciled peace.

Now he was violating it with his constant campaign-
ing: *Sell the house and move to the Haven.* (You sit, you
sit—there too you could sit like a stone.) He was making
of her a battleground where old grievances tore. (Turn
on your ear button—I am talking.) And stubbornly
she resisted—so that from wheedling, reasoning, manipu-
lation, it was bitterness he now started with.

And it came to where every happening lashed up a
quarrel.

"I will sell the house anyway," he flung at her one
night. "I am putting it up for sale. There will be a
way to make you sign."

The television blared, as always it did on the evenings
he stayed home, and as always it reached her only as
noise. She did not know if the tumult was in her or outside. Snap! she turned the sound off. "Shadows," she
whispered to him, pointing to the screen, "look, it is
only shadows." And in a scream: "Did you say that you
will sell the house? Look at me, not at that. I am no
shadow. You cannot sell without me."

"Leave on the television. I am watching."

"Like Paulie, like Jenny, a four-year-old. Staring at
shadows. *You cannot sell the house.*"

"I will. We are going to the Haven. There you would
not hear the television when you do not want it. I

could sit in the social room and watch. You could lock yourself up to smell your unpleasantness in a room by yourself—for who would want to come near you?"

"No, no selling." A whisper now.

"The television is shadows. Mrs. Enlightened! Mrs. Cultured! A world comes into your house—and it is shadows. People you would never meet in a thousand lifetimes. Wonders. When you were four years old, yes, like Paulie, like Jenny, did you know of Indian dances, alligators, how they use bamboo in Malaya? No, you scratched in your dirt with the chickens and thought Olshana was the world. Yes, Mrs. Unpleasant, I will sell the house, for there better can we be rid of each other than here."

She did not know if the tumult was outside, or in her. Always a ravening inside, a pull to the bed, to lie down, to succumb.

"Have you thought maybe Ma should let a doctor have a look at her?" asked their son Paul after Sunday dinner, regarding his mother crumpled on the couch, instead of, as was her custom, busying herself in Nancy's kitchen.

"Why not the President too?"

"Seriously, Dad. This is the third Sunday she's lain down like that after dinner. Is she that way at home?"

"A regular love affair with the bed. Every time I start to talk to her."

Good protective reaction, observed Nancy to herself. The workings of hos-til-ity.

"Nancy could take her. I just don't like how she looks. Let's have Nancy arrange an appointment."

"You think she'll go?" regarding his wife gloomily. "All right, we have to have doctor bills, we have to have doctor bills." Loudly: "Something hurts you?"

She startled, looked to his lips. He repeated: "Mrs. Take It Easy, something hurts?"

"Nothing. . . . Only you."

"A woman of honey. That's why you're lying down?"

"Soon I'll get up to do the dishes, Nancy."

"Leave them, Mother, I like it better this way."

"Mrs. Take It Easy, Paul says you should start ballet. You should go to see a doctor and ask: how soon can you start ballet?"

"A doctor?" she begged. "Ballet?"

"We were talking, Ma," explained Paul, "you don't seem any too well. It would be a good idea for you to see a doctor for a checkup."

"I get up now to do the kitchen. Doctors are bills and foolishness, my son. I need no doctors."

"At the Haven," he could not resist pointing out, "a doctor is *not* bills. He lives beside you. You start to sneeze, he is there before you open up a Kleenex. You can be sick there for free, all you want."

"Diarrhea of the mouth, is there a doctor to make you dumb?"

"Ma. Promise me you'll go. Nancy will arrange it."

"It's all of a piece when you think of it," said Nancy, "the way she attacks my kitchen, scrubbing under every

cup hook, doing the inside of the oven so I can't enjoy
Sunday dinner, knowing that half-blind or not, she's
going to find every speck of dirt. . . ."

"Don't, Nancy, I've told you—it's the only way she
knows to be useful. What did the *doctor* say?"

"A real fatherly lecture. Sixty-nine is young these
days. Go out, enjoy life, find interests. Get a new hearing aid, this one is antiquated. Old age is sickness only
if one makes it so. Geriatrics, Inc."

"So there was nothing physical."

"Of course there was. How can you live to yourself
like she does without there being? Evidence of a kidney
disorder, and her blood count is low. He gave her a diet,
and she's to come back for follow-up and lab work.
. . . But he was clear enough: Number One prescription—start living like a human being. . . . When I
think of your dad, who could really play the invalid
with that arthritis of his, as active as a teenager, and
twice as much fun. . . ."

"You didn't tell me the doctor says your sickness is
in you, how you live." He pushed his advantage. "Life
and enjoyments you need better than medicine. And
this diet, how can you keep it? To weigh each morsel
and scrape away each bit of fat, to make this soup, that
pudding. There, at the Haven, they have a dietician,
they would do it for you."

She is silent.

"You would feel better there, I know it," he says
gently. "There there is life and enjoyments all around."

"What is the matter, Mr. Importantbusy, you have

no card game or meeting you can go to?"—turning her
face to the pillow.

For a while he cut his meetings and going out, fussed
over her diet, tried to wheedle her into leaving the
house, brought in visitors:

"I should come to a fashion tea. I should sit and look
at pretty babies in clothes I cannot buy. This is pleasure?"

"Always you are better than everyone else. The doctor said you should go out. Mrs. Brem comes to you
with goodness and you turn her away."

"Because *you* asked her to, she asked me."

"They won't come back. People you need, the doctor
said. Your own cousins I asked; they were willing to
come and make peace as if nothing had happened. . . ."

"No more crushers of people, pushers, hypocrites,
around me. No more in *my* house. You go to them
if you like."

"Kind he is to visit. And you, like ice."

"A babbler. All my life around babblers. Enough!"

"She's even worse, Dad? Then let her stew a while,"
advised Nancy. "You can't let it destroy you; it's a
psychological thing, maybe too far gone for any of us
to help."

So he let her stew. More and more she lay silent in
bed, and sometimes did not even get up to make the

meals. No longer was the tongue-lashing inevitable if he left the coffee cup where it did not belong, or forgot to take out the garbage or mislaid the broom. The birds grew bold that summer and for once pocked the pears, undisturbed.

A bellyful of bitterness and every day the same quarrel in a new way and a different old grievance the quarrel forced her to enter and relive. And the new torment: I am not really sick, the doctor said it, then why do I feel so sick?

One night she asked him: "You have a meeting tonight? Do not go. Stay . . . with me."

He had planned to watch "This Is Your Life," but half sick himself from the heavy heat, and sickening therefore the more after the brooks and woods of the Haven, with satisfaction he grated:

"Hah, Mrs. Live Alone And Like It wants company all of a sudden. It doesn't seem so good the time of solitary when she was a girl exile in Siberia. 'Do not go. Stay with me.' A new song for Mrs. Free As A Bird. Yes, I am going out, and while I am gone chew this aloneness good, and think how you keep us both from where if you want people, you do not need to be alone."

"Go, go. All your life you have gone without me."

After him she sobbed curses he had not heard in years, old-country curses from their childhood: Grow, oh shall you grow like an onion, with your head in the ground. Like the hide of a drum shall you be, beaten in life, beaten in death. Oh shall you be like a chandelier, to hang, and to burn. . . .

She was not in their bed when he came back. She

lay on the cot on the sun porch. All week she did not
speak or come near him; nor did he try to make peace
or care for her.

He slept badly, so used to her next to him. After all
the years, old harmonies and dependencies deep in their
bodies; she curled to him, or he coiled to her, each
warmed, warming, turning as the other turned, the
nights a long embrace.

It was not the empty bed or the storm that woke him,
but a faint singing. *She* was singing. Shaking off the
drops of rain, the lightning riving her lifted face, he
saw her so; the cot covers on the floor.

"This is a private concert?" he asked. "Come in, you
are wet."

"I can breathe now," she answered; "my lungs are
rich." Though indeed the sound was hardly a breath.

"Come in, come in." Loosing the bamboo shades.
"Look how wet you are." Half helping, half carrying
her, still faint-breathing her song.

A Russian love song of fifty years ago.

He had found a buyer, but before he told her, he
called together those children who were close enough
to come. Paul, of course, Sammy from New Jersey,
Hannah from Connecticut, Vivi from Ohio.

With a kindling of energy for her beloved visitors,
she arrayed the house, cooked and baked. She was not
prepared for the solemn after-dinner conclave, they too
probing in and tearing. Her frightened eyes watched
from mouth to mouth as each spoke.

His stories were eloquent and funny of her refusal to
go back to the doctor; of the scorned invitations; of her

stubborn silence or the bile "like a Niagara"; of her contrariness: "If I clean it's no good how I cleaned; if I don't clean, I'm still a master who thinks he has a slave."

(Vinegar he poured on me all his life; I am well marinated; how can I be honey now?)

Deftly he marched in the rightness for moving to the Haven; their money from social security free for visiting the children, not sucked into daily needs and into the house; the activities in the Haven for him; but mostly the Haven for *her:* her health, her need of care, distraction, amusement, friends who shared her interests.

"This does offer an outlet for Dad," said Paul; "he's always been an active person. And economic peace of mind isn't to be sneezed at, either. I could use a little of that myself."

But when they asked: "And you, Ma, how do you feel about it?" could only whisper:

"For him it is good. It is not for me. I can no longer live between people."

"You lived all your life *for* people," Vivi cried.

"Not with." Suffering doubly for the unhappiness on her children's faces.

"You have to find some compromise," Sammy insisted. "Maybe sell the house and buy a trailer. After forty-seven years there's surely some way you can find to live in peace."

"There is no help, my children. Different things we need."

"Then live alone!" He could control himself no longer. "I have a buyer for the house. Half the money for you, half for me. Either alone or with me to the

Haven. You think I can live any longer as we are doing now?"

"Ma doesn't have to make a decision this minute, however you feel, Dad," Paul said quickly, "and you wouldn't want her to. Let's let it lay a few months, and then talk some more."

"I think I can work it out to take Mother home with me for a while," Hannah said. "You both look terrible, but especially you, Mother. I'm going to ask Phil to have a look at you."

"Sure," cracked Sammy. "What's the use of a doctor husband if you can't get free service out of him once in a while for the family? And absence might make the heart . . . you know."

"There was something after all," Paul told Nancy in a colorless voice. "That was Hannah's Phil calling. Her gall bladder. . . . Surgery."

"Her *gall* bladder. If that isn't classic. 'Bitter as gall' —talk of psychosom——"

He stepped closer, put his hand over her mouth, and said in the same colorless, plodding voice. "We have to get Dad. They operated at once. The cancer was everywhere, surrounding the liver, everywhere. They did what they could . . . at best she has a year. Dad . . . we have to tell him."

2

Honest in his weakness when they told him, and that she was not to know. "I'm not an actor. She'll know right away by how I am. Oh that poor woman. I am old

too, it will break me into pieces. Oh that poor woman.
She will spit on me: 'So my sickness was how I live.'
Oh Paulie, how she will be, that poor woman. Only she
should not suffer. . . . I can't stand sickness, Paulie,
I can't go with you."

But went. And play-acted.

"A grand opening and you did not even wait for me.
. . . A good thing Hannah took you with her."

"Fashion teas I needed. They cut out what tore in
me; just in my throat something hurts yet. . . . Look!
so many flowers, like a funeral. Vivi called, did Hannah
tell you? And Lennie from San Francisco, and Clara;
and Sammy is coming." Her gnome's face pressed hap-
pily into the flowers.

It is impossible to predict in these cases, but once
over the immediate effects of the operation, she should
have several months of comparative well-being.

The money, where will come the money?

Travel with her, Dad. Don't take her home to the
old associations. The other children will want to
see her.

The money, where will I wring the money?

Whatever happens, she is not to know. No, you
can't ask her to sign papers to sell the house; nothing
to upset her. Borrow instead, then after. . . .

*I had wanted to leave you each a few dollars to
make life easier, as other fathers do. There will be
nothing left now. (Failure! you and your "business
is exploitation." Why didn't you make it when it
could be made?—Is that what you're thinking,
Sammy?)*

Sure she's unreasonable, Dad—but you have to stay with her; if there's to be any happiness in what's left of her life, it depends on you.

Prop me up, children, think of me, too. Shuffled, chained with her, bitter woman. No Haven, and the little money going. . . . How happy she looks, poor creature.

The look of excitement. The straining to hear everything (the new hearing aid turned full). Why are you so happy, dying woman?

How the petals are, fold on fold, and the gladioli color. The autumn air.

Stranger grandsons, tall above the little gnome grandmother, the little spry grandfather. Paul in a frenzy of picture-taking before going.

She, wandering the great house. Feeling the books; laughing at the maple shoemaker's bench of a hundred years ago used as a table. The ear turned to music.

"Let us go home. See how good I walk now." "One step from the hospital," he answers, "and she wants to fly. Wait till Doctor Phil says."

"Look—the birds too are flying home. Very good Phil is and will not show it, but he is sick of sickness by the time he comes home."

"Mrs. Telepathy, to read minds," he answers; "read mine what it says: when the trunks of medicines become a suitcase, then we will go."

The grandboys, they do not know what to say to us. . . . Hannah, she runs around here, there, when is there time for herself?

Let us go home. Let us go home.

Musing; gentleness—*but for the incidents of the rabbi
in the hospital, and of the candles of benediction.*

Of the rabbi in the hospital:

Now tell me what happened, Mother.

From the sleep I awoke, Hannah's Phil, and he
stands there like a devil in a dream and calls me by
name. I cannot hear. I think he prays. Go away,
please, I tell him, I am not a believer. Still he stands,
while my heart knocks with fright.

You scared *him,* Mother. He thought you were
delirious.

Who sent him? Why did he come to *me?*

It is a custom. The men of God come to visit those
of their religion they might help. The hospital makes
up the list for them—race, religion—and you are on
the Jewish list.

Not for rabbis. At once go and make them change.
Tell them to write: Race, human; Religion, none.

And of the candles of benediction:

Look how you have upset yourself, Mrs. Excited
Over Nothing. Pleasant memories you should leave.

Go in, go back to Hannah and the lights. Two
weeks I saw candles and said nothing. But she asked
me.

So what was so terrible? She forgets you never did,
she asks you to light the Friday candles and say the
benediction like Phil's mother when she visits. If the
candles give her pleasure, why shouldn't she have
the pleasure?

Not for pleasure she does it. For emptiness. Because his family does. Because all around her do.

That is not a good reason too? But you did not hear her. For heritage, she told you. For the boys, from the past they should have tradition.

Superstition! From our ancestors, savages, afraid of the dark, of themselves: mumbo words and magic lights to scare away ghosts.

She told you: how it started does not take away the goodness. For centuries, peace in the house it means.

Swindler! does she look back on the dark centuries? Candles bought instead of bread and stuck into a potato for a candlestick? Religion that stifled and said: in Paradise, woman, you will be the footstool of your husband, and in life—poor chosen Jew— ground under, despised, trembling in cellars. And cremated. And cremated.

This is religion's fault? You think you are still an orator of the 1905 revolution? Where are the pills for quieting? Which are they?

Heritage. How have we come from our savage past, how no longer to be savages—this to teach. To look back and learn what humanizes—this to teach. To smash all ghettos that divide us—not to go back, not to go back—this to teach. Learned books in the house, will humankind live or die, and she gives to her boys—superstition.

Hannah that is so good to you. Take your pill, Mrs. Excited For Nothing, swallow.

Heritage! But when did I have time to teach? Of Hannah I asked only hands to help.

Swallow.

Otherwise—musing; gentleness.

Not to travel. To go home.

The children want to see you. We have to show them you are as thorny a flower as ever.

Not to travel.

Vivi wants you should see her new baby. She sent the tickets—airplane tickets—a Mrs. Roosevelt she wants to make of you. To Vivi's we have to go.

A new baby. How many warm, seductive babies. She holds him stiffly, *away* from her, so that he wails. And a long shudder begins, and the sweat beads on her forehead.

"Hush, shush," croons the grandfather, lifting him back. "You should forgive your grandmamma, little prince, she has never held a baby before, only seen them in glass cases. Hush, shush."

"You're tired, Ma," says Vivi. "The travel and the noisy dinner. I'll take you to lie down."

(*A long travel from, to, what the feel of a baby evokes.*)

In the airplane, cunningly designed to encase from motion (no wind, no feel of flight), she had sat severely and still, her face turned to the sky through which they cleaved and left no scar.

So this was how it looked, the determining, the crucial sky, and this was how man moved through it, remote above the dwindled earth, the concealed human life. Vulnerable life, that could scar.

There was a steerage ship of memory that shook

across a great, circular sea: clustered, ill human beings; and through the thick-stained air, tiny fretting waters in a window round like the airplane's—sun round, moon round. (The round thatched roofs of Olshana.) Eye round—like the smaller window that framed distance the solitary year of exile when only her eyes could travel, and no voice spoke. And the polar winds hurled themselves across snows trackless and endless and white —like the clouds which had closed together below and hidden the earth.

Now they put a baby in her lap. Do not ask me, she would have liked to beg. Enough the worn face of Vivi, the remembered grandchildren. I cannot, cannot. . . .

Cannot what? Unnatural grandmother, not able to make herself embrace a baby.

She lay there in the bed of the two little girls, her new hearing aid turned full, listening to the sound of the children going to sleep, the baby's fretful crying and hushing, the clatter of dishes being washed and put away. They thought she slept. Still she rode on.

It was not that she had not loved her babies, her children. The love—the passion of tending—had risen with the need like a torrent; and like a torrent drowned and immolated all else. But when the need was done— oh the power that was lost in the painful damming back and drying up of what still surged, but had nowhere to go. Only the thin pulsing left that could not quiet, suffering over lives one felt, but could no longer hold nor help.

On that torrent she had borne them to their own lives, and the riverbed was desert long years now. Not

there would she dwell, a memoried wraith. Surely that
was not all, surely there was more. Still the springs, the
springs were in her seeking. Somewhere an older power
that beat for life. Somewhere coherence, transport,
meaning. If they would but leave her in the air now
stilled of clamor, in the reconciled solitude, to journey
on.

And they put a baby in her lap. Immediacy to embrace, and the breath of *that* past: warm flesh like this
that had claims and nuzzled away all else and with lovely
mouths devoured; hot-living like an animal—intensely
and now; the turning maze; the long drunkenness; the
drowning into needing and being needed. Severely she
looked back—and the shudder seized her again, and the
sweat. Not that way. Not there, not now could she, not
yet. . . .

And all that visit, she could not touch the baby.

"Daddy, is it the . . . sickness she's like that?" asked
Vivi. "I was so glad to be having the baby—for her. I
told Tim, it'll give her more happiness than anything,
being around a baby again. And she hasn't played with
him once."

He was not listening, "Aahh little seed of life, little
charmer," he crooned, "Hollywood should see you. A
heart of ice you would melt. Kick, kick. The future
you'll have for a ball. In 2050 still kick. Kick for your
grandaddy then."

Attentive with the older children; sat through their
performances (command performance; we command you

to be the audience); helped Ann sort autumn leaves to find the best for a school program; listened gravely to Richard tell about his rock collection, while her lips mutely formed the words to remember: *igneous, sedimentary, metamorphic;* looked for missing socks, books, and bus tickets; watched the children whoop after their grandfather who knew how to tickle, chuck, lift, toss, do tricks, tell secrets, make jokes, match riddle for riddle. (Tell me a riddle, Grammy. I know no riddles, child.) Scrubbed sills and woodwork and furniture in every room; folded the laundry; straightened drawers; emptied the heaped baskets waiting for ironing (while he or Vivi or Tim nagged: You're supposed to rest here, you've been sick) but to none tended or gave food—and could not touch the baby.

After a week she said: "Let us go home. Today call about the tickets."

"You have important business, Mrs. Inahurry? The President waits to consult with you?" He shouted, for the fear of the future raced in him. "The clothes are still warm from the suitcase, your children cannot show enough how glad they are to see you, and you want home. There is plenty of time for home. We cannot be with the children at home."

"Blind to around you as always: the little ones sleep four in a room because we take their bed. We are two more people in a house with a new baby, and no help."

"Vivi is happy so. The children should have their grandparents a while, she told to me. I should have my mommy and daddy. . . ."

"Babbler and blind. Do you look at her so tired?

How she starts to talk and she cries? I am not strong
enough yet to help. Let us go home."

(To reconciled solitude.)

*For it seemed to her the crowded noisy house was
listening to her, listening for her. She could feel it like
a great ear pressed under her heart. And everything
knocked: quick constant raps: let me in, let me in.*

*How was it that soft reaching tendrils also became
blows that knocked?*

C'mon, Grandma, I want to show you. . . .

Tell me a riddle, Grandma. (*I know no riddles.*)

Look, Grammy, he's so dumb he can't even find his
hands. (Dody and the baby on a blanket over the
fermenting autumn mould.)

I made them—for you. (Ann) (Flat paper dolls with
aprons that lifted on scalloped skirts that lifted on
flowered pants; hair of yarn and great ringed questioning eyes.)

Watch me, Grandma. (Richard snaking up the tree,
hanging exultant, free, with one hand at the top.
Below Dody hunching over in pretend-cooking.)
(*Climb too, Dody, climb and look.*)

Be my nap bed, Grammy. (The "No!" too late.)
Morty's abandoned heaviness, while his fingers ladder
up and down her hearing-aid cord to his drowsy
chant: eentsiebeentsiespider. (*Children trust.*)

It's to start off your own rock collection, Grandma.
That's a trilobite fossil, 200 million years old (millions

of years on a boy's mouth) and that one's obsidian,
black glass.

Knocked and knocked.

Mother, I *told* you the teacher said we had to bring
it back all filled out this morning. Didn't you even
ask Daddy? Then tell *me* which plan and I'll check
it: evacuate or stay in the city or wait for you to come
and take me away. (Seeing the look of straining to
hear.) It's for Disaster, Grandma. (*Children trust.*)

Vivi in the maze of the long, the lovely drunkenness.
The old old noises: baby sounds; screaming of a
mother flayed to exasperation; children quarreling;
children playing; singing; laughter.

And Vivi's tears and memories, spilling so fast, half
the words not understood.

She had started remembering out loud deliberately,
so her mother would know the past was cherished, still
lived in her.

Nursing the baby: My friends marvel, and I tell them,
oh it's easy to be such a cow. I remember how beautiful
my mother seemed nursing my brother, and the milk
just flows. . . . Was that Davy? It must have been
Davy. . . .

Lowering a hem: How did you ever . . . when I
think how you made everything we wore . . . Tim,
just think, seven kids and Mommy sewed everything
. . . do I remember you sang while you sewed? That
white dress with the red apples on the skirt you fixed

over for me, was it Hannah's or Clara's before it was mine?

Washing sweaters: Ma, I'll never forget, one of those days so nice you washed clothes outside; one of the first spring days it must have been. The bubbles just danced while you scrubbed, and we chased after, and you stopped to show us how to blow our own bubbles with green onion stalks . . . you always. . . .

"Strong onion, to still make you cry after so many years," her father said, to turn the tears into laughter.

While Richard bent over his homework: Where is it now, do we still have it, the Book of the Martyrs? It always seemed so, well—exalted, when you'd put it on the round table and we'd all look at it together; there was even a halo from the lamp. The lamp with the beaded fringe you could move up and down; they're in style again, pulley lamps like that, but without the fringe. You know the book I'm talking about, Daddy, the Book of the Martyrs, the first picture was a bust of Spartacus . . . Socrates? I wish there was something like that for the children, Mommy, to give them what you. . . . (And the tears splashed again.)

(What I intended and did not? Stop it, daughter, stop it, leave that time. And he, the hyprocrite, sitting there with tears in his eyes—it was nothing to you then, nothing.)

. . . The time you came to school and I almost died of shame because of your accent and because I knew you knew I was ashamed; how could I? . . . Sammy's harmonica and you danced to it once, yes you did, you and Davy squealing in your arms. . . . That time you bundled us up and walked us down to the railway station to stay the night 'cause it was heated and we didn't have any coal, that winter of the strike, you didn't think I remembered that, did you, Mommy? . . . How you'd call us out to see the sunsets. . . .

Day after day, the spilling memories. Worse now, questions, too. Even the grandchildren: Grandma, in the olden days, when you were little. . . .

It was the afternoons that saved.

While they thought she napped, she would leave the mosaic on the wall (of children's drawings, maps, calendars, pictures, Ann's cardboard dolls with their great ringed questioning eyes) and hunch in the girls' closet on the low shelf where the shoes stood, and the girls' dresses covered.

For that while she would painfully sheathe against the listening house, the tendrils and noises that knocked, and Vivi's spilling memories. Sometimes it helped to braid and unbraid the sashes that dangled, or to trace the pattern on the hoop slips.

Today she had jacks and children under jet trails to forget. Last night, Ann and Dody silhouetted in the window against a sunset of flaming man-made clouds of jet trail, their jacks ball accenting the peaceful noise of dinner being made. Had she told them, yes she had told them of how they played jacks in her village though there was no ball, no jacks. Six stones, round and flat, toss them out, the seventh on the back of the hand, toss, catch and swoop up as many as possible, toss again. . . .

Of stones (repeating Richard) there are three kinds:

earth's fire jetting; rock of layered centuries; crucibled new out of the old (*igneous, sedimentary, metamorphic*). But there was that other—frozen to black glass, never to transform or hold the fossil memory . . . (let not my seed fall on stone). There was an ancient man who fought to heights a great rock that crashed back down eternally—eternal labor, freedom, labor . . . (stone will perish, but the word remain). And you, David, who with a stone slew, screaming: Lord, take my heart of stone and give me flesh

Who was screaming? Why was she back in the common room of the prison, the sun motes dancing in the shafts of light, and the informer being brought in, a prisoner now, like themselves. And Lisa leaping, yes, Lisa, the gentle and tender, biting at the betrayer's jugular. Screaming and screaming.

No, it is the children screaming. Another of Paul and Sammy's terrible fights?

In Vivi's house. Severely: you are in Vivi's house.

Blows, screams, a call: "Grandma!" For her? Oh please not for her. Hide, hunch behind the dresses deeper. But a trembling little body hurls itself beside her—surprised, smothered laughter, arms surround her neck, tears rub dry on her cheek, and words too soft to understand whisper into her ear (Is this where you hide too, Grammy? It's my secret place, we have a secret now).

And the sweat beads, and the long shudder seizes.

It seemed the great ear pressed inside now, and the knocking. "We have to go home," she told him, "I grow ill here."

"It's your own fault, Mrs. Bodybusy, you do not rest, you do too much." He raged, but the fear was in his eyes. "It was a serious operation, they told you to take care. . . . All right, we will go to where you can rest."

But where? Not home to death, not yet. He had thought to Lennie's, to Clara's; beautiful visits with each of the children. She would have to rest first, be stronger. If they could but go to Florida—it glittered before him, the never-realized promise of Florida. California: of course. (The money, the money, dwindling!) Los Angeles first for sun and rest, then to Lennie's in San Francisco.

He told her the next day. "You saw what Nancy wrote: snow and wind back home, a terrible winter. And look at you—all bones and a swollen belly. I called Phil: he said: 'A prescription, Los Angeles sun and rest.' "

She watched the words on his lips. "You have sold the house," she cried, "that is why we do not go home. That is why you talk no more of the Haven, why there is money for travel. After the children you will drag me to the Haven."

"The Haven! Who thinks of the Haven any more? Tell her, Vivi, tell Mrs. Suspicious: a prescription, sun and rest, to make you healthy. . . . And how could I sell the house without *you?*"

At the place of farewells and greetings, of winds of coming and winds of going, they say their good-byes.

They look back at her with the eyes of others before them: Richard with her own blue blaze; Ann with the nordic eyes of Tim; Morty's dreaming brown of a great-grandmother he will never know; Dody with the laughing eyes of him who had been her springtide love (who stands beside her now); Vivi's, all tears.

The baby's eyes are closed in sleep.

Good-bye, my children.

3

It is to the back of the great city he brought her, to the dwelling places of the cast-off old. Bounded by two lines of amusement piers to the north and to the south, and between a long straight paving rimmed with black benches facing the sand—sands so wide the ocean is only a far fluting.

In the brief vacation season, some of the boarded stores fronting the sands open, and families, young people and children, may be seen. A little tasselled tram shuttles between the piers, and the lights of roller coasters prink and tweak over those who come to have sensation made in them.

The rest of the year it is abandoned to the old, all else boarded up and still; seemingly empty, except the occasional days and hours when the sun, like a tide, sucks them out of the low rooming houses, casts them onto the benches and sandy rim of the walk—and sweeps them into decaying enclosures once again.

A few newer apartments glint among the low bleached squares. It is in one of these Lennie's Jeannie has arranged their rooms. "Only a few miles north and south people pay hundreds of dollars a month for just this gorgeous air, Grandaddy, just this ocean closeness."

She had been ill on the plane, lay ill for days in the unfamiliar room. Several times the doctor came by— left medicine she would not take. Several times Jeannie drove in the twenty miles from work, still in her Visiting Nurse uniform, the lightness and brightness of her like a healing.

"Who can believe it is winter?" he asked one morning. "Beautiful it is outside like an ad. Come, Mrs. Invalid, come to taste it. You are well enough to sit in here, you are well enough to sit outside. The doctor said it too."

But the benches were encrusted with people, and the sands at the sidewalk's edge. Besides, she had seen the far ruffle of the sea: "there take me," and though she leaned against him, it was she who led.

Plodding and plodding, sitting often to rest, he grumbling. Patting the sand so warm. Once she scooped up a handful, cradling it close to her better eye; peered, and flung it back. And as they came almost to the brink and she could see the glistening wet, she sat down, pulled off her shoes and stockings, left him and began to run. "You'll catch cold," he screamed, but the sand in his shoes weighed him down—he who had always been the agile one—and already the white spray creamed her feet.

He pulled her back, took a handkerchief to wipe off the wet and the sand. "Oh no," she said, "the sun will dry," seized the square and smoothed it flat, dropped on it a mound of sand, knotted the kerchief corners and tied it to a bag—"to look at with the strong glass" (for the first time in years explaining an action of hers)—and lay down with the little bag against her cheek, looking toward the shore that nurtured life as it first crawled toward consciousness the millions of years ago.

He took her one Sunday in the evil-smelling bus, past flat miles of blister houses, to the home of relatives. Oh what is this? she cried as the light began to smoke and the houses to dim and recede. Smog, he said, everyone knows but you. . . . Outside he kept his arms about her, but she walked with hands pushing the heavy air as if to open it, whispered: who has done this? sat down suddenly to vomit at the curb and for a long while refused to rise.

One's age as seen on the altered face of those known in youth. Is this they he has come to visit? This Max and Rose, smooth and pleasant, introducing them to polite children, disinterested grandchildren, "the whole family, once a month on Sundays. And why not? We have the room, the help, the food."

Talk of cars, of houses, of success: this son that, that daughter this. And *your* children? Hastily skimped over, the intermarriages, the obscure work—"my doctor son-in-law, Phil"—all he has to offer. She silent in a corner. (Car-sick like a baby, he explains.) Years since he has taken her to visit anyone but the children, and old apprehensions prickle: "no incidents," he silently begs, "no incidents." He itched to tell them. "A very sick woman," significantly, indicating her with his eyes, "a very sick woman." Their restricted faces did not react. "Have you thought maybe she'd do better at Palm Springs?" Rose asked. "Or at least a nicer section of the beach, nicer people, a pool." Not to have to say "money" he said instead: "would she have sand to look at through a magnifying glass?" and went on, detail after detail, the old habit betraying of parading the queerness of her for laughter.

After dinner—the others into the living room in men- or women-clusters, or into the den to watch TV —the four of them alone. She sat close to him, and did not speak. Jokes, stories, people they had known, beginning of reminiscence, Russia fifty-sixty years ago. Strange words across the Duncan Phyfe table: *hunger; secret meetings; human rights; spies; betrayals; prison; escape*—interrupted by one of the grandchildren: "Commercial's on; any Coke left? Gee, you're missing a real hair-raiser." And then a granddaughter (Max proudly: "look at her, an American queen") drove them home on her way back to U.C.L.A. No incident—except that there had been no incidents.

The first few mornings she had taken with her the magnifying glass, but he would sit only on the benches, so she rested at the foot, where slatted bench shadows fell, and unless she turned her hearing aid down, other voices invaded.

Now on the days when the sun shone and she felt well enough, he took her on the tram to where the benches ranged in oblongs, some with tables for checkers or cards. Again the blanket on the sand in the striped shadows, but she no longer brought the magnifying glass. He played cards, and she lay in the sun and looked towards the waters; or they walked—two blocks down to the scaling hotel, two blocks back—past chili-hamburger stands, open-doored bars, Next -to- New and perpetual rummage sale stores.

Once, out of the aimless walkers, slow and shuffling like themselves, someone ran unevenly towards them, embraced, kissed, wept: "dear friends, old friends." A friend of *hers*, not his: Mrs. Mays who had lived next door to them in Denver when the children were small.

Thirty years are compressed into a dozen sentences; and the present, not even in three. All is told: the children scattered; the husband dead; she lives in a room two blocks up from the sing hall—and points to the domed auditorium jutting before the pier. The leg? phlebitis; the heavy breathing? that, one does not ask. She, too, comes to the benches each day to sit. And tomorrow, tomorrow, are they going to the community sing? Of course he would have heard of it, everybody goes—the big doings they wait for all week. They have never been? She will come to them for dinner tomorrow and they will all go together.

So it is that she sits in the wind of the singing, among the thousand various faces of age.

She had turned off her hearing aid at once they came into the auditorium—as she would have wished to turn off sight.

One by one they streamed by and imprinted on her— and though the savage zest of their singing came voicelessly soft and distant, the faces still roared—the faces densened the air—chorded into

children-chants, mother-croons, singing of the chained
love serenades, Beethoven storms, mad Lucia's scream
drunken joy-songs, keens for the dead, work-singing

> *while from floor to balcony to dome a bare-footed*
> *sore-covered little girl threaded the sound-*
> *thronged tumult, danced her ecstasy of grimace*
> *to flutes that scratched at a cross-roads village*
> *wedding*

Yes, faces became sound, and the sound became faces;
and faces and sound became weight—pushed, pressed

"Air"—her hands claw his.

"Whenever I enjoy myself. . . ." Then he saw the
gray sweat on her face. "Here. Up. Help me, Mrs.
Mays," and they support her out to where she can gulp
the air in sob after sob.

"A doctor, we should get for her a doctor."

"Tch, it's nothing," says Ellen Mays, "I get it all the
time. You've missed the tram; come to my place. Fix
your hearing aid, honey . . . close . . . tea. My view.
See, she *wants* to come. Steady now, that's how." Adding
mysteriously: "Remember your advice, easy to keep your
head above water, empty things float. Float."

The singing a fading march for them, tall woman
with a swollen leg, weaving little man, and the swollen
thinness they help between.

The stench in the hall: mildew? decay? "We sit and

rest then climb. My gorgeous view. We help each other
and here   we   are."

The stench along into the slab of room. A washstand
for a sink, a box with oilcloth tacked around for a cupboard, a three-burner gas plate. Artificial flowers, colorless with dust. Everywhere pictures foaming: wedding,
baby, party, vacation, graduation, family pictures. From
the narrow couch under a slit of window, sure enough
the view: lurching rooftops and a scallop of ocean heav-
ing, preening, twitching under the moon.

"While the water heats. Excuse me . . . down the
hall." Ellen Mays has gone.

"You'll live?" he asks mechanically, sat down to feel
his fright; tried to pull her alongside.

She pushed him away. "For air," she said; stood
clinging to the dresser. Then, in a terrible voice:

After a lifetime of room. Of many rooms.

Shhh.

You remember how she lived. Eight children. And
now one room   like a coffin.

She pays rent!

Shrinking the life of her   into one room   like a
coffin   Rooms and rooms like this   I lie on the quilt
and hear them talk

Please, Mrs. Orator-without-Breath.

Once you went for coffee   I walked   I saw   A
Balzac   a Chekhov to write it   Rummage   Alone   On
scraps

Better old here than in the old country!

On scraps   Yet they sang like   like   Wondrous!

Humankind   one has to believe So strong   for what?
To rot   not grow?

Your poor lungs beg you. They sob between each
word.

Singing.   Unused the life in them. She in this
poor room   with her   pictures   Max   You   The
children   Everywhere unused the life   And who
has meaning?   Century after century   still all in
us   not to grow?

Coffins, rummage, plants: sick woman. Oh lay down.
We will get for you the doctor.

"And when will it end. Oh, *the end.*" *That* night-
mare thought, and this time she writhed, crumpled
against him, seized his hand (for a moment again the
weight, the soft distant roaring of humanity) and on
the strangled-for breath, begged: "Man . . . we'll destroy ourselves?"

And looking for answer—in the helpless pity and
fear for her (for *her*) that distorted his face—she understood the last months, and knew that she was dying.

4

"Let us go home," she said after several days.

"You are in training for a cross-country run? That
is why you do not even walk across the room? Here,
like a prescription Phil said, till you are stronger from
the operation. You want to break doctor's orders?"

She saw the fiction was necessary to him, was silent;

then: "At home I will get better. If the doctor here
says?"

"And winter? And the visits to Lennie and to Clara?
All right," for he saw the tears in her eyes, "I will write
Phil, and talk to the doctor."

Days passed. He reported nothing. Jeannie came and
took her out for air, past the boarded concessions, the
hooded and tented amusement rides, to the end of the
pier. They watched the spent waves feeding the new,
the gulls in the clouded sky; even up where they sat,
the wind-blown sand stung.

She did not ask to go down the crooked steps to the
sea.

Back in her bed, while he was gone to the store, she
said: "Jeannie, this doctor, he is not one I can ask
questions. Ask him for me, can I go home?"

Jeannie looked at her, said quickly: "Of course, poor
Granny. You want your own things around you, don't
you? I'll call him tonight. . . . Look, I've something
to show you," and from her purse unwrapped a large
cookie, intricately shaped like a little girl. "Look at the
curls—can you hear me well, Granny?—and the darling
eyelashes. I just came from a house where they were
baking them."

"The dimples, there in the knees," she marveled,
holding it to the better light, turning, studying, "like
art. Each singly they cut, or a mold?"

"Singly," said Jeannie, "and if it is a child only the
mother can make them. Oh Granny, it's the likeness
of a real little girl who died yesterday—Rosita. She was
three years old. *Pan del Muerto,* the Bread of the Dead.

It was the custom in the part of Mexico they came from."

Still she turned and inspected. "Look, the hollow in the throat, the little cross necklace. . . . I think for the mother it is a good thing to be busy with such bread. You know the family?"

Jeannie nodded. "On my rounds. I nursed. . . . Oh Granny, it is like a party; they play songs she liked to dance to. The coffin is lined with pink velvet and she wears a white dress. There are candles. . . ."

"In the house?" Surprised, "They keep her in the house?"

"Yes," said Jeannie, "and it *is* against the health law. The father said it will be sad to bury her in this country; in Oaxaca they have a feast night with candles each year; everyone picnics on the graves of those they loved until dawn."

"Yes, Jeannie, the living must comfort themselves." And closed her eyes.

"You want to sleep, Granny?"

"Yes, tired from the pleasure of you. I may keep the Rosita? There stand it, on the dresser, where I can see; something of my own around me."

In the kitchenette, helping her grandfather unpack the groceries, Jeannie said in her light voice:

"I'm resigning my job, Grandaddy."

"Ah, the lucky young man. Which one is he?"

"Too late. You're spoken for." She made a pyramid of cans, unstacked, and built again.

"Something is wrong with the job?"

"With me. I can't be"—she searched for the word—
"What they call professional enough. I let myself feel
things. And tomorrow I have to report a family. . . ."
The cans clicked again. "It's not that, either. I just don't
know what I want to do, maybe go back to school, maybe
go to art school. I thought if you went to San Francisco
I'd come along and talk it over with Momma and
Daddy. But I don't see how you can go. She wants to
go home. She asked me to ask the doctor."

The doctor told her himself. "Next week you may
travel, when you are a little stronger." But next week
there was the fever of an infection, and by the time that
was over, she could not leave the bed—a rented hospital
bed that stood beside the double bed he slept in alone
now.

Outwardly the days repeated themselves. Every other
afternoon and evening he went out to his newfound
cronies, to talk and play cards. Twice a week, Mrs. Mays
came. And the rest of the time, Jeannie was there.

By the sickbed stood Jeannie's FM radio. Often into
the room the shapes of music came. She would lie
curled on her side, her knees drawn up, intense in
listening (Jeannie sketched her so, coiled, convoluted
like an ear), then thresh her hand out and abruptly
snap the radio mute—still to lie in her attitude of
listening, concealing tears.

Once Jeannie brought in a young Marine to visit, a
friend from high-school days she had found wandering
near the empty pier. Because Jeannie asked him to,

gravely, without self-consciousness, he sat himself cross-legged on the floor and performed for them a dance of his native Samoa.

Long after they left, a tiny thrumming sound could be heard where, in her bed, she strove to repeat the beckon, flight, surrender of his hands, the fluttering footbeats, and his low plaintive calls.

Hannah and Phil sent flowers. To deepen her pleasure, he placed one in her hair. "Like a girl," he said, and brought the hand mirror so she could see. She looked at the pulsing red flower, the yellow skull face; a desolate, excited laugh shuddered from her, and she pushed the mirror away—but let the flower burn.

The week Lennie and Helen came, the fever returned. With it the excited laugh, and incessant words. She, who in her life had spoken but seldom and then only when necessary (never having learned the easy, social uses of words), now in dying, spoke incessantly.

In a half-whisper: "Like Lisa she is, your Jeannie. Have I told you of Lisa who taught me to read? Of the highborn she was, but noble in herself. I was sixteen; they beat me; my father beat me so I would not go to her. It was forbidden, she was a Tolstoyan. At night, past dogs that howled, terrible dogs, my son, in the snows of winter to the road, I to ride in her carriage like a lady, to books. To her, life was holy, knowledge was holy, and she taught me to read. They hung her. Everything that happens one must try to understand why. She killed one who betrayed many. Because of betrayal, betrayed all she lived and believed. In one minute she killed, before my eyes (there is so much blood in a human being, my son), in prison with me. All that happens, one must try to understand.

"The name?" Her lips would work. "The name that was their pole star; the doors of the death houses fixed to open on it; I read of it my year of penal servitude. Thuban!" very excited, "Thuban, in ancient Egypt the pole star. Can you see, look out to see it, Jeannie, if it swings around *our* pole star that seems to *us* not to move.

"Yes, Jeannie, at your age my mother and grandmother had already buried children . . . yes, Jeannie, it is more than oceans between Olshana and you . . . yes, Jeannie, they danced, and for all the bodies they had they might as well be chickens, and indeed, they scratched and flapped their arms and hopped.

"And Andrei Yefimitch, who for twenty years had never known of it and never wanted to know, said as if he wanted to cry: but why my dear friend this malicious laughter?" Telling to herself half-memorized phrases from her few books. "Pain I answer with tears and cries, baseness with indignation, meanness with repulsion . . . for life may be hated or wearied of, but never despised."

Delirious: "Tell me, my neighbor, Mrs. Mays, the pictures never lived, but what of the flowers? Tell them who ask: no rabbis, no ministers, no priests, no speeches, no ceremonies: ah, false—let the living comfort themselves. Tell Sammy's boy, he who flies, tell him to go to Stuttgart and see where Davy has no grave. And what? . . . And what? where millions have no graves—save air."

In delirium or not, wanting the radio on; not seeming

to listen, the words still jetting, wanting the music on. Once, silencing it abruptly as of old, she began to cry, unconcealed tears this time. "You have pain, Granny?" Jeannie asked.

"The music," she said, "still it is there and we do not hear; knocks, and our poor human ears too weak. What else, what else we do not hear?"

Once she knocked his hand aside as he gave her a pill, swept the bottles from her bedside table: "no pills, let me feel what I feel," and laughed as on his hands and knees he groped to pick them up.

Nighttimes her hand reached across the bed to hold his.

A constant retching began. Her breath was too faint for sustained speech now, but still the lips moved:

When no longer necessary   to injure others
Pick   pick pick   Blind chicken
As a human being   responsibility

"David!" imperious, "Basin!" and she would vomit, rinse her mouth, the wasted throat working to swallow, and begin the chant again.

She will be better off in the hospital now, the doctor said.

He sent the telegrams to the children, was packing her suitcase, when her hoarse voice startled. She had roused, was pulling herself to sitting.

"Where now?" she asked. "Where now do you drag me?"

"You do not even have to have a baby to go this

time," he soothed, looking for the brush to pack. "Remember, after Davy you told me—worthy to have a baby for the pleasure of the ten-day rest in the hospital?"

"Where now? Not home yet?" Her voice mourned. "Where *is* my home?"

He rose to ease her back. "The doctor, the hospital," he started to explain, but deftly, like a snake, she had slithered out of bed and stood swaying, propped behind the night table.

"Coward," she hissed, "runner."

"You stand," he said senselessly.

"To take me there and run. Afraid of a little vomit."

He reached her as she fell. She struggled against him, half slipped from his arms, pulled herself up again.

"Weakling," she taunted, "to leave me there and run. Betrayer. All your life you have run."

He sobbed, telling Jeannie. "A Marilyn Monroe to run for her virtue. Fifty-nine pounds she weighs, the doctor said, and she beats at me like a Dempsey. Betrayer, she cries, and I running like a dog when she calls; day and night, running to her, her vomit, the bedpan. . . ."

"She needs you, Grandaddy," said Jeannie. "Isn't that what they call love? I'll see if she sleeps, and if she does, poor worn-out darling, we'll have a party, you and I: I brought us rum babas."

They did not move her. By her bed now stood the tall hooked pillar that held the solutions—blood and dextrose—to feed her veins. Jeannie moved down the hall to take over the sickroom, her face so radiant, her grandfather asked her once: "you are in love?" (Shameful the joy, the pure overwhelming joy from being with her grandmother; the peace, the serenity that breathed.) "My darling escape," she answered incoherently, "my darling Granny"—as if that explained.

Now one by one the children came, those that were able. Hannah, Paul, Sammy. Too late to ask: and what did you learn with your living, Mother, and what do we need to know?

Clara, the eldest, clenched:

Pay me back, Mother, pay me back for all you took from me. Those others you crowded into your heart. The hands I needed to be for you, the heaviness, the responsibility.

Is this she? Noises the dying make, the crablike hands crawling over the covers. The ethereal singing.

She hears that music, that singing from childhood; forgotten sound—not heard since, since. . . . And the hardness breaks like a cry: Where did we lose each other, first mother, singing mother?

Annulled: the quarrels, the gibing, the harshness between; the fall into silence and the withdrawal.

I do not know you, Mother. Mother, I never knew you.

Lennie, suffering not alone for her who was dying, but for that in her which never lived (for that which in him might never come to live. From him too, unspoken words: *good-bye Mother who taught me to mother my-self.*

Not Vivi, who must stay with her children; not Davy, but he is already here, having to die again with *her* this time, for the living take their dead with them when they die.

Light she grew, like a bird, and, like a bird, sound bubbled in her throat while the body fluttered in agony. Night and day, asleep or awake (though indeed there was no difference now) the songs and the phrases leaping.

And he, who had once dreaded a long dying (from fear of himself, from horror of the dwindling money) now desired her quick death profoundly, for *her* sake. He no longer went out, except when Jeannie forced him; no longer laughed, except when, in the bright kitchenette, Jeannie coaxed his laughter (and she, who seemed to hear nothing else, would laugh too, conspiratorial wisps of laughter).

Light, like a bird, the fluttering body, the little claw hands, the beaked shadow on her face; and the throat, bubbling, straining.

He tried not to listen, as he tried not to look on the face in which only the forehead remained familiar, but trapped with her the long nights in that little room, the sounds worked themselves into his consciousness, with their punctuation of death swallows, whimpers, gurglings.

Even in reality (swallow) *life's lack of it*
Slaveships deathtrains clubs   eeenough
The bell   summon what enables

78,000 in one minute (whisper of a scream) *78,000 human beings   we'll destroy ourselves?*

"Aah, Mrs. Miserable," he said, as if she could hear, "all your life working, and now in bed you lie, servants to tend, you do not even need to call to be tended, and still you work. Such hard work it is to die? Such hard work?"

The body threshed, her hand clung in his. A melody, ghost-thin, hovered on her lips, and like a guilty ghost, the vision of her bent in listening to it, silencing the record instantly he was near. Now, heedless of his presence, she floated the melody on and on.

"Hid it from me," he complained, "how many times you listened to remember it so?" And tried to think when she had first played it, or first begun to silence her few records when he came near—but could reconstruct nothing. There was only this room with its tall hooked pillar and its swarm of sounds.

No man one   except through others
Strong   with the not yet   in the now
Dogma dead   war dead   one country

"It helps, Mrs. Philosopher, words from books? It helps?" And it seemed to him that for seventy years she had hidden a tape recorder, infinitely microscopic, within her, that it had coiled infinite mile on mile, trapping every song, every melody, every word read, heard, and spoken—and that maliciously she was playing back only what said nothing of him, of the children, of their intimate life together.

"Left us indeed, Mrs. Babbler," he reproached, "you who called others babbler and cunningly saved your words. A lifetime you tended and loved, and now not a word of us, for us. Left us indeed? Left me."

And he took out his solitaire deck, shuffled the cards loudly, slapped them down.

Lift high banner of reason (tatter of an orator's voice) *justice   freedom   light*
  Humankind   life worthy capacities
  Seeks (blur of shudder) *belong human being*

"Words, words," he accused, "and what human beings did *you* seek around you, Mrs. Live Alone, and what humankind think worthy?"

Though even as he spoke, he remembered she had not always been isolated, had not always wanted to be alone (as he knew there had been a voice before this gossamer one; before the hoarse voice that broke from silence to lash, make incidents, shame him—a girl's voice of eloquence that spoke their holiest dreams). But again he could reconstruct, image, nothing of what had been before, or when, or how, it had changed.

Ace, queen, jack. The pillar shadow fell, so, in two tracks; in the mirror depths glistened a moonlike blob, the empty solution bottle. And it worked in him: *of reason and justice and freedom . . . Dogma dead:* he remembered the full quotation, laughed bitterly. "Hah, good you do not know what you say; good Victor Hugo died and did not see it, his twentieth century."

Deuce, ten, five. Dauntlessly she began a song of their youth of belief:

> *These things shall be, a loftier race*
> *than e'er the world hath known shall rise*

with flame of freedom in their souls
and light of knowledge in their eyes

King, four, jack "In the twentieth century, hah!"

> *They shall be gentle, brave and strong*
> *to spill no drop of blood, but dare*
> *all . . .*
>> *on earth and fire and sea and air*

"To spill no drop of blood, hah! So, cadaver, and you too, cadaver Hugo, 'in the twentieth century ignorance will be dead, dogma will be dead, war will be dead, and for all mankind one country—of fulfilment?' Hah!"

> *And every life* (long strangling cough) *shall*
>> *be a song*

The cards fell from his fingers. Without warning, the bereavement and betrayal he had sheltered—compounded through the years—hidden even from himself —revealed itself,
> uncoiled,
> released,
> *sprung*

and with it the monstrous shapes of what had actually happened in the century.

A ravening hunger or thirst seized him. He groped into the kitchenette, switched on all three lights, piled a tray—"you have finished your night snack, Mrs. Cadaver, now I will have mine." And he was shocked at the tears that splashed on the tray.

"Salt tears. For free. I forgot to shake on salt?"

Whispered: "Lost, how much I lost."

Escaped to the grandchildren whose childhoods were childish, who had never hungered, who lived unravaged by disease in warm houses of many rooms, had all the school for which they cared, could walk on any street, stood a head taller than their grandparents, towered above—beautiful skins, straight backs, clear straightforward eyes. "Yes, you in Olshana," he said to the town of sixty years ago, "they would look nobility to you."

And was this not the dream then, come true in ways undreamed? he asked.

And are there no other children in the world? he answered, as if in her harsh voice.

And the flame of freedom, the light of knowledge?

And the drop, to spill no drop of blood?

And he thought that at six Jeannie would get up and it would be his turn to go to her room and sleep, that he could press the buzzer and she would come now; that in the afternoon Ellen Mays was coming, and this time they would play cards and he could marvel at how rouge can stand half an inch on the cheek; that in the evening the doctor would come, and he could beg him to be merciful, to stop the feeding solutions, to let her die.

To let her die, and with her their youth of belief out of which her bright, betrayed words foamed; stained words, that on her working lips came stainless.

Hours yet before Jeannie's turn. He could press the

buzzer and wake her to come now; he could take a pill, and with it sleep; he could pour more brandy into his milk glass, though what he had poured was not yet touched.

Instead he went back, checked her pulse, gently tended with his knotty fingers as Jeannie had taught.

She was whimpering; her hand crawled across the covers for his. Compassionately he enfolded it, and with his free hand gathered up the cards again. Still was there thirst or hunger ravening in him.

That world of their youth—dark, ignorant, terrible with hate and disease—how was it that living in it, in the midst of corruption, filth, treachery, degradation, they had not mistrusted man nor themselves; had believed so beautifully, so . . . falsely?

"Aaah, children," he said out loud, "how we believed, how we belonged." And he yearned to package for each of the children, the grandchildren, for everyone, *that joyous certainty, that sense of mattering, of moving and being moved, of being one and indivisible with the great of the past, with all that freed, ennobled.* Package it, stand on corners, in front of stadiums and on crowded beaches, knock on doors, give it as a fabled gift.

"And why not in cereal boxes, in soap packages?" he mocked himself. "Aah. You have taken my senses, cadaver."

Words foamed, died unsounded. Her body writhed; she made kissing motions with her mouth. (Her lips moving as she read, poring over the Book of the Martyrs, the magnifying glass superimposed over the heavy eyeglasses.) *Still she believed?* "Eva!" he whispered. "Still you believed? You lived by it? These Things Shall Be?"

"One pound soup meat," she answered distinctly, "one soup bone."

"My ears heard you. Ellen Mays was witness: 'Humankind . . . one has to believe.' " Imploringly: "Eva!"

"Bread, day-old." She was mumbling. "Please, in a wooden box . . . for kindling. The thread, hah, the thread breaks. Cheap thread"—and a gurgling, enormously loud, began in her throat.

"I ask for stone; she gives me bread—day-old." He pulled his hand away, shouted: "Who wanted questions? Everything you have to wake?" Then dully, "Ah, let me help you turn, poor creature."

Words jumbled, cleared. In a voice of crowded terror: "Paul, Sammy, don't fight.

"Hannah, have I ten hands?

"How can I give it, Clara, how can I give it if I don't have?"

"You lie," he said sturdily, "there was joy too." Bitterly: "Ah how cheap you speak of us at the last."

As if to rebuke him, as if her voice had no relationship with her flailing body, she sang clearly, beautifully, a school song the children had taught her when they were little; begged:

"Not look   my hair   where they cut. . . ."

(The crown of braids shorn.) And instantly he left the mute old woman poring over the Book of the Martyrs; went past the mother treading at the sewing machine, singing with the children; past the girl in her wrinkled prison dress, hiding her hair with scarred hands, lifting to him her awkward, shamed, imploring eyes of love; and took her in his arms, dear, personal, fleshed, in all the heavy passion he had loved to rouse from her.

"Eva!"

Her little claw hand beat the covers. How much, how much can a man stand? He took up the cards, put them down, circled the beds, walked to the dresser, opened, shut drawers, brushed his hair, moved his hand bit by bit over the mirror to see what of the reflection he could blot out with each move, and felt that at any moment he would die of what was unendurable. Went to press the buzzer to wake Jeannie, looked down, saw on Jeannie's sketch pad the hospital bed, with *her;* the double bed alongside, with him; the tall pillar feeding into her veins, and their hands, his and hers, clasped, feeding each other. And as if he had been instructed he went to his bed, lay down, holding the sketch (as if it could shield against the monstrous shapes of loss, of betrayal, of death) and with his free hand took hers back into his.

So Jeannie found them in the morning.

That last day the agony was perpetual. Time after time it lifted her almost off the bed, so they had to fight to hold her down. He could not endure and left the room; wept as if there never would be tears enough.

Jeannie came to comfort him. In her light voice she said: Grandaddy, Grandaddy don't cry. She is not there, she promised me. On the last day, she said she would go back to when she first heard music, a little girl on

the road of the village where she was born. She promised
me. It is a wedding and they dance, while the flutes so
joyous and vibrant tremble in the air. Leave her there,
Grandaddy, it is all right. She promised me. Come back,
come back and help her poor body to die.

For my mother, my father,
and
Two of that generation
Seevya and Genya
Infinite, dauntless, incorruptible

Death deepens the wonder